PRAISE

MW01181134

WINNER for science fiction in the 2011 Independent Publisher's Book Awards.

"An exciting read that should prove hard to put down." ~ *MidWest Book Review*

"Science can be a boon to humanity, but it can also be its bane. *The Presence* is a science fiction thriller set in a future where reality is something manufactured by corporations. Sonny Chaco is charged with finding something that resembles law in this world. As he tails one billionaire CEO who may have made those billions with a bit foul tactics, he finds that the reality manufacture industry is more tumultuous than he could ever hope, and that throwing some romance only complicates the complicated. *The Presence* is an EXCITING READ that should prove HARD TO PUT DOWN."

~ *Midwest Book Review*

"It was a FAST READ and I enjoyed the trip that it took me on. It's one of the better hard Sci-Fi books I've read in a long time, and Paul Black is an author I'm looking forward to seeing more from!"

~ *Jordan Mason, themoviepool.com.*

"Author Paul Black brings a fresh look to the near future fiction writing genre."

~ *PearlSnapDiscount.com*

"*The Presence* is fast-paced and WELL WRITTEN. Paul pulls futuristic tech into a believable and seamless world."

~ *Darcia Helle, author Quiet Furry Books*

WINNER for genre fiction in the
Writer's Digest's International Book Awards.

Gold and Silver medalist for science fiction,
ForeWord Magazine's Book of the Year.

"Dallas writer Paul Black makes his first foray into the world of science fiction with *The Tels*. It's a HIGHLY ORIGINAL novel set in the near future and IT MOVES AT LIGHTNING SPEED. Mr. Black has quite an imagination and puts it to good use. The MIND-BENDING PLOT centers on Jonathan Kortel, who is approached by a shadowy group called the Tels, who covet his telekinetic gifts. The ENSUING ACTION IS BIZARRE enough to read like something straight out of *The X-Files*."

~ *Steve Powers, Dallas Morning News*

"(*The Tels*) is WRITTEN SO SPLENDIDLY, at times I forgot I was reading science fiction – with the emphasis on fiction. The characters are realistic, and the hero is someone you relate to, worry about and wonder if he's going to be able to cope with the reality that is set before him. This is definitely ONE OF THE BEST SCIENCE FICTION NOVELS I've ever read...the BOOK IS REMARKABLE."

~ *Marilyn Meredith, Writer's Digest's 11th Annual Book Awards*

"...*Soulware* was a BRILLIANTLY EMBROIDERED STORY, mixing science and fiction in a plausible and entertaining way...I absolutely LOVED THIS BOOK!"

~ *Ismael Manzano, G-POP.net*

"A riveting science fiction novel...an imaginatively skilled storyteller."

"This story by Paul Black is as STRONG AND WELL WRITTEN as any of the stories of my heroes: Robert Heinlein, Isaac Asimov, Andre Norton, or Anne McCaffrey. He is one of those writers that we who worship this genre look for every time we pick up the novel of an author who is new to us...The CHARACTERS COME ALIVE for you. You feel right along with them. You can believe the decisions they make. And best of all, nothing is clear-cut and simple. The story brings us to a strong ending while leaving us with the desire for more...I recommend *The Tels* to every lover of sci-fi. Good work, Paul! Welcome to my bookshelves!"

~ John Strange, thecityweb.com

"Paul Black's ENGAGING PROSE promises big things for the future...."

~ Writer's Notes Magazine

"...a GREAT READ, full of suspense and action...."

~ Dallas Entertainment Guide

"A RIVETING science fiction novel by a gifted author...*The Tels* would prove a popular addition to any community library Science Fiction collection and documents Paul Black as an IMAGINATIVELY SKILLED STORYTELLER of the first order. Also very highly recommended is the newly published second volume in the *Tels* series, *Soulware*, which continues the adventures of Jonathan Kortel in the world of tomorrow."

~ Midwest Book Review

"The Tels is an addictive read... manages to capture the reader in the first ten pages...The Tels has it all."

"Black rises above the Trekkie laser tag spastics found in your typical sci-fi novels resting on the grocery store racks. His sensibilities broaden from machine gun testosterone to discreet fatherhood, from errant sexuality to wry humor. HE DELIVERS A CHARGE OF VENTURE RARELY FOUND IN FIRST-TIME WRITERS. And *THE TELS* HITS THE MARK as a solid adventure serial, leaving you hanging for the next publication."

~ *Brian Adams, Collegian*

"*The Tels* is an ADDICTIVE READ from first-time novelist Paul Black, a promising new storyteller on the sci-fi scene. He manages to capture the reader in the first ten pages. He introduces us to a set of intriguing characters in a totally believable possible future. There is a grittiness and sensuality to his writing that pours out of every word in the book. Whether it's his description of the preparation of a good meal, the seduction of a beautiful woman, or a fight to the death, *THE TELS* HAS IT ALL. Even people who don't read sci-fi will want to read this book. The action is great and would make one hell of a movie. Is Hollywood listening? Paul Black has a winner on his hands. I can hardly wait for the next installment."

~ *Cynthia A., About Towne, ITCN*

"*Soulware* doesn't miss a beat as it continues Jonathan's story, the story of his quest to find out exactly who he really is and why the Tels are so interested in him. The ending makes it clear that there's more to come, and readers who crave their science-fiction with a hint of weirdness can look forward to the next book in the series."

~ *Steve Powers, Dallas Morning News*

the presence

A NOVEL BY

paul black

NOVEL INSTINCTS

Programmable Matter is a trademark of
The Programmable Matter Corporation.

NOVEL INSTINCTS PUBLISHING
6008 Ross Avenue
Dallas, Texas 75206
www.novelinstincts.com and www.paulblackbooks.com

This book can be ordered on the web at most major retail sites including www.barnesandnoble.com and www.amazon.com.

ISBN: 978-0-9726007-4-3
1. Fiction / Science Fiction / High Tech 2. Fiction / Near-Future
Library of Congress Control Number: 2010934982
Printed in the United States of America.
10 9 8 7 6 5 4 3 2 1

Cover photo: PhotoDisc /GettyOne.
Author photo by Jeff Baker, www.jeffbakerphoto.

TO MY WRITER'S GROUP

~

For keeping me on the path.

The greater good

"**DEJA**?!"

Deja Moriarty sensed her boss's beckon somewhere at the periphery of her consciousness. She left her virtual researching and peeled the Netgear from her head. Its microfiber-optics uncoupled into techno dreadlocks that glowed prismatic at their ends. She cautiously peered over her cubicle.

"Ah, there you are!" Bishop Green's anger was clearly in professional check because *Life's a Bitch* had dropped to a 22.0

share in the weekly ratings, now making it the second-most-watched program in AztecaNet's prime-time lineup. Which meant the second-most-watched program on the planet. Which also meant his bid for the old Kennedy compound, out in the Hamptons, would have to hold at its present number. Since his earnings were directly tied to the Net ratings, the people who labored under Green had come to accept his emotional swings as part of the package. There had been other success stories, but nothing compared to Green's. His prolific output of hit programming not only exceeded shareholder expectations, but also garnered him accolades usually bestowed on producers twice his age. Bishop Green was definitely AztecaNet's undisputed "it" boy.

Deja passed a hand through her electric blond hair and strutted toward him with all the confidence her new assistant producer title could bring.

"Be a dear and get Sotheby's on the line for me. And if you're headed that way ..." Green raised his coffee cup.

"What kind of sugar day are we having?" Deja asked, irritated with his lack of acceptance of her new role.

Green thought for a second, then a sly grin grew across his face. "Triple."

"Oh! One of *those* days."

"Yes, it is," Green said, then suddenly shifted mien and announced to anyone in earshot, "and if we don't get *Life's a Bitch* back up to number one, there'll be a housecleaning like you've never seen!"

Life's a Bitch was Green's brainchild and had perched at the top of the ratings for over a year. Its concept was simple: destroy an ordinary life as a ruthlessly brutal world looks on. Nanocameras disguised as houseflies provided a world audience with an unfettered view of the destruction, while AztecaNet's patents on the camera's technology ensured its reign as the leader in reality-based programming. It also gave new meaning to an old phrase.

In the beginning, the plan was to leave individuals destroyed. But after the pilot season's first unsuspecting contestant, Leonard Smotts, decided to reduce himself to a puddle of matter by eating the butt end of a Light-Force, AztecaNet's lawyers decided that revealing the prank and restoring a person's life might be the preferred option. The finale had been completely reworked with a digitally processed Leonard morphed into a happy ending. Litigation with his family was still pending, but if the numbers held, final payoff to keep the Smott family's contractual silence would be a drop in the bucket compared to the revenues from *Life's a Bitch*.

"Three sugars, please," Deja ordered into the system pad at the snack dispenser, but then thought better. "Wait! Make that four." The dispenser's door slid aside and presented a steaming ceramic mug of coffee, specially blended to Bishop Green's genetic profile. Only she had access to his codes.

Deja had worked with Green as his assistant since his producer beginnings on the soapy Net drama *All of Their Days*, where he would have probably gone unnoticed if it weren't for the sudden exit of its head producer to the Chelsea Clinton Clinic. When Green took control of *All of Their Days*, it was floundering somewhere near the bottom of the ratings. And since the suits at AztecaNet considered it fodder for a demographic comprised mainly of those left floundering by the economic shift of the Biolution, they never noticed Green's decision to "tweak" the formula when he fired all the writers.

Green felt the audience of the Net was better suited to dictating the comings and goings of the simple folk of Waterville. By switching *All of Their Days* to an interactive format, he created a promotion manager's wet dream and offered weekly contests for the best scripts, which, conveniently, were judged by Green and his favorite assistant.

Slowly, *All of Their Days* ratings began to climb as Green and Deja allowed a tasteless, insomniac audience to drive the daily actions of their show's characters. Being a late Friday night product meant talent was barely "C" level, comprised mostly of young actors who would do practically anything for the mere possibility of Network exposure. So when Deja presented Green with a script written by a particularly horny housewife from Manchester, England, who suggested the show's leads go ahead and give in to their characters' carnal passions, Green announced to his stunned associates there had been a shift in direction for their little corner of the Net.

Since the show's leads were sleeping with each other off camera anyway, the two actors merged business with pleasure and gave their worldwide fan base a season they would never forget. It was weeks before Network censors caught on, but by then *All of Their Days* was in the Top 10. It became an underground hit that redefined the late-night soap genre and catapulted Green to phenom status with many of the boardroom suits. It also brought Green to the attention of AztecaNet's parent company, Grupo TVid Azteca, and its chairman, Alberto Goya.

Deja handed Green his coffee. "I need to show you this bit of info I've dug up on Billy Bob—"

"Ray," he corrected, reviewing his Netpad. "Billy *Ray*."

"Well, whatever his name is, our little Texas boy has a whole other offshore account he's been diverting gobs of cash to for the last ten months."

Green looked up mid-sip and raised an eyebrow. "Mistress?"

"Oh, *yeah*."

Green smiled around the edge of his cup and took a gulp. "That's why I love you, Dej. You always have your priorities in the right place." He turned and headed toward studio 2B, but stopped and glanced back. He pointed with the cup. "Oh, and ah, nice coffee, love ... just right."

*   *   *

"Good night, Miss Moriarty."

Deja looked up at the intern.

"Working late?"

Deja grinned tersely and returned to her Netport, its cerulean glow the sole light in her cubical. The kid sulked away.

"You alone?" Sonny Chaco's image filled the screen.

Deja glanced about. "Yeah, it's just me and the data."

"You running that security program I gave you?"

She rolled her eyes. "Yes, Sonny, I am."

"Okay, don't get upset."

"I don't like all this spy business."

Chaco's holoimage quivered out from Deja's Netport as he sat in the cramped confines of his office, deep in the lower levels of the National Security Agency. He relaxed and gave Deja that grin, just like he did the first time they had met at the National Netcasters Convention a year earlier.

"Look, if you're uncomfortable–"

"It's not that," Deja said, not listening to her better self. "It's just ..." She tentatively bit at one of her nails, and its color retreated into the cuticle.

"What, you feel like you're ratting on your boss?"

"He's not technically my boss, but yeah ... it feels weird."

"What you're doing is brave, and it's for the greater good.

"I know, but this is my company. My future's tied up here."

"Taking down a suit like Goya isn't going to faze a

corporation as big as Azteca. It might even help. Did you ever think of that?"

"Well, no."

"Let's make this the last one for a while, all right? And to celebrate, why don't you jump a shuttle up here and let me treat you to dinner at Fusion." Chaco leaned forward, and his image grew to the edges of the screen's holo parameters.

"I don't think they have my gen file anymore," she said.

"They do. I've already checked."

Deja matched Chaco's action, knowing her image was enlarging at his end. She touched her index finger to his holo lips and narrowed her eyes into sexy slits. "You've got this all worked out, don't you."

"And what if I do?"

"Then this won't be the only thing you'll be getting this weekend." She slowly grinned and clicked the Send button.

Too late

TODAY should have been the day that he stopped throwing up. He lifts his head from the trashcan's stench and sees his image in a store window. A curry-colored drop falls from his chin in a thick, slow motion. He had been warned. SI: Sensory Inundation – probably from the shift in travel.

He straightens and wipes his mouth with the sleeve of his coat, then centers himself in the black vibration that continuously emanates from the pavement. He studies the people who walk past ambivalently and succumbs to the realization that the populace of his new home is sadder than he ever imagined. He has spent the better part of his life studying for the assignment. They all do. But his studies, he now feels, have not prepared him for what he will face.

He looks up at the blanket of permanently ashen clouds and tries to understand what happened. The city where he was placed is the nation's largest and is considered the cradle of everything current. Its urban dementia seems to merge into endless patterns of gray skies, liquor advertising, and parking garages slowly spreading like industrial lichen to the southernmost point a thousand miles away. The sheer mass of the sprawl isn't what consumes him. It is something else – something more elusive.

The noise.

Day and night, its subtle presence is relentless, humming its processed merger of a trillion tonal discharges into what, he has been told, is affectionately called "the hum." He fears it will take some getting used to, but he will. He'll have to.

Most everything was set up before his arrival. He has plenty of money, which was imbedded into the financial system five years prior so that its presence would be solid and unassuming – enough to live on for the rest of his life. But some essentials have been left out. "Be inventive" was the directive.

He enters the little bodega. "Yo, leather-boy, looking or buying?" asks the Asian clerk, who has categorized him by his shoes. An old man watches him with eyes that seem to distill every detail of his actions in even ocular movements. He can barely tell the clerk's eyes have shifted, because the dark brown slits don't easily reveal the direction they might be focusing.

"Looking," he answers, trying not to reveal his complete naiveté with a culture he has barely greeted.

"Shitfuck," the clerk says so under his breath that it sounds more like some ancient dialect than New American.

He walks the aisles and studies everything in the store, from the types of products to the styles of design. One thing this culture doesn't lack is variety. They have a seemingly endless appetite for goods and entertainment, which can be produced, he concludes, in solid, liquid, virtual, or pharmaceutical forms. And if a need can't be bought in a store, it might be found in any of the thousands of "entertainment cafes" that fill the cracks of their cultural landscape.

"If you're goin' to hang this long, what's your deno?" The Asian is shaking a large wooden spoon at him through a thick haze of stir-fry and cigarette smoke.

Deno? He deduces that the clerk wants to know his name, which is yet another thing his instructors failed to provide. He recalls their teachings.

The new technological revolution, or "Biolution," as the media termed it, was a blessing and a curse. It caused whole industries to vanish, yet promoted, in a kind of sick display of reverse karma, a whole new wave of decadence and global promiscuity. Its fusion of organic peptides and nanotechnology erased, among other things, many of the medical threats from a century earlier. Now many people could afford the luxury to destroy vital organs without worry. New liver, new lungs, new pancreas, a new attitude – modern medicine could regenerate whatever was needed, quickly and affordably. Cradle to grave, the Biolution force-fed the middle-class a steady diet of misery wrapped in festively colored mediocrity.

"Are jou deaf, too?" the clerk asks.

His focus settles on the dozens of cigarette packs competing for attention behind the protection of the counter's armored plexi. "Hmm?" he says, having clearly heard the clerk, yet wanting to test his retail tolerance.

"*Ko-chu-pado*!"

The pack with the red triangle seems very popular.

"*Yumago*," he replies.

The clerk's eyes open with surprise. Then his lips part and form a smile that causes the skin of his face to fractal into hundreds of creases. The clerk appears to age before him.

"Jou spreak Korean!" the clerk declares, still aging. "So, what's your deno?"

"Marl," he answers, fixating on the pack with the red triangle. He needs a name, and the directive was: Be inventive.

"Where jou learn to spreak Korean?"

"I've been around," Marl answers in the best street speak

his memory can bring forth. The inflection is off, but with a few minutes of exposure, it will be easily corrected.

The tinkling of chimes signals the cramming of another customer into the store; Mr. Korean's shop begins to fill with people getting their late-night meal supplements or bottles of their favorite entertainment. The woman entering is wrapped by an expensive biocoat whose collar demands she accept a measured amount of pain in service of fashion. Even her movement is different, which suggests that she lives a life free from the trappings that burden the other customers. They keep their distance while she glides through the store.

As Marl studies her, he has a sad feeling that she is faking it – that her act is a put-on and probably not her idea. He stands at the front counter: still, silent, rapt like the other men by her exquisite figure and hair that seems to be evolving from a different lineage than her makeup. Her coat's living fabric senses the change in environment and relaxes. She slips through the store collecting a small contingent of party essentials: two bottles of Polish potato vodka, one bottle of standard meal sup, a bag of hydro-bars, a deodorant microchip, and a vid. A classic. She enters the checkout line, and a man in front of her steps back. The woman moves so in sync that Marl wonders if she is precognitive. She nudges a box of candy off its wire shelf and glances at her backside like it has acted on its own.

"Oh," she says.

No, he figures, this girl is definitely a package deal. Probably grown to a customer's specs in the vats of the Lesser Antilles, where binders of girls are churned up from the voodoo science that lurks near the fringes of the Biolution. She catches his stare.

"*Casablanca?*" he asks, trying not to grace her acknowledgement with a shift in posture.

She glances into her basket, and a small grin forms at the edges of her full lips. The pattern of her gloss shifts. "Have you seen it?"

"Yes." He instantly calls up all he can on the film and its actors.

"What's your favorite part?" she presses.

His memory rallies. "When Ilsa asks Sam to play it again."

She peels back her sunglasses and reveals a set of striking green eyes with rings of hot orange circling the irises. The pupils narrow like a cat's. Custom. Probably aftermarket. And if he wasn't so enthralled with how they were set above a pair of dimples he can only describe as perfect, he might have missed the slight discoloration of the bruise. Its mottled purple travels the length of the lid and conspicuously disappears into a delicate layer of makeup.

But he doesn't.

The flinch is instinctive.

She quickly replaces the glasses, which reset with a sucking sound. "Yeah," she says, edgy. "That and the airplane scene are my faves." She disconnects.

"A night for Bogie ..."

She places her basket on the floor and quickly walks toward the store's exit. The doors slide open, and her coat senses the rush of cold night air and tightens at the neck, cuffs, and thighs. Marl and the clerk watch her disappear into the fray that has descended on this part of the city for a night of whatever gets them off. The doors jitter before slamming shut.

"She's crustom!" Mr. Korean says, pointing after her with his big wooden spoon. He returns to the sizzling contents of a large wok he has been nursing behind the counter.

"Who's not?" Marl says, still staring.

"She's not natwural."

An odd statement coming from a man Marl suspects has a new set of regen'd lungs. He compassionately eyes the old Korean.

"Ah, *dong-mongo*!" And the clerk throws his attention back into the wok.

Intrigued, Marl exits the shop on the off chance that the woman, Miss Unnatural, might actually be in sight. Emerging, he finds himself in an endless sea of discarded faces, all perched atop their winter coats in a desperate attempt at comfort. The crowd moves along the viscera of the sidewalk like gray waste forced ahead by a peristaltic emotion he can only label "despair." In the week since his arrival, he has sensed a connection forming. The people fascinate him, because each one is a stunning collection of eukaryotic history, all traceable to one singular start buried deep in a lineage that spans the millennia. He searches their faces and begins feeling a tremendous pressure, like a physical declaration of the intense importance of his assignment. Then a shift carves through his being, destroying the resolve that his foundation rested upon. Suddenly, he wonders if he has arrived too late, like a doctor realizing there is nothing left to do.

He becomes overwhelmed, and the nausea rises again.

Staggering, Marl leans heavily against the glass of Mr. Korean's shop. He feels a hand at his shoulder.

"Hey, are you all right? You don't look so good."

The stranger's eyes are calm, and his grip full of care.

Marl straightens and struggles to smile.

"You gotta watch yourself. New York can bite you in the ass if you're not careful." The stranger winks and slips back into the flow.

De acuerdo.

THE courier measured his pace as he trotted down the long corridor. A minute too soon would be as damaging as a minute too late. He glanced at his watch. *11:58:04 a.m.* He slowed to a walk.

12:00:00 p.m.

"Good afternoon, Stephen," a disembodied female voice said.

The courier took the final step and leaned toward the reader panel. "Good afternoon, Ms. Sanchez."

"Are you packed today?"

"Yes, ma'am, I am."

The courier could feel the HVAC kick in, creating a faint hum somewhere at the edge of his hearing. The hallway was empty, the nondescript system panel the only element embellishing the stark white walls. The muscles of his neck tightened in anticipation.

"I'm ready," the woman said.

The courier released the optic fiber from its cell with a swipe of his card and caught it as it popped free. A complex task reduced to an artfully simple move by hundreds of deliveries. He removed his sunglasses and snapped the fiber into the connector below his left eye. Widening his stance, the courier closed his eyes and prepared for the transfer of data.

"You've styled your hair differently."

The courier opened his eyes. "Yes, ma'am, I have."

"*Muy atractivo.*"

"*Gracias, señora.*"

There was a sound that resembled a laugh. "I think I like the new Stephen."

The courier smiled.

"Are we ready?"

"Yes, ma'am."

"Let's begin."

The courier took in a deep breath, and his vision dissolved.

*   *   *

Oscar Pavia was sitting comfortably in one of the overstuffed leather sofas that defined a meeting area near the front of his boss's office.

"Mr. Pavia, Ms. Sanchez is here," a smooth female voice declared.

"Thank you, Maria," he said.

Hidden by the opening door, Pavia watched Isabel Sanchez walk into the room. He could always tell the importance of a file by where his boss would stand. By the windows was bad. By the desk was good. By the bar was personal. Sanchez placed the sliver of organic polymer next to the desk's Netport. Alberto Goya turned from one of the large windows that ran the length of the office and eyed it.

"*Gracias*," he said politely.

"*De nada*." Sanchez turned but froze when she saw Pavia.

He smiled, forcing the genuineness.

Sanchez acknowledged him with a slight, awkward tilt of her head, then hurried from the room.

"Alberto," Pavia said. "When are you going to enter the modern age?"

Goya looked up from slipping the file into his Netport. "When it's secure, my friend."

Alberto Goya was a tall, native Mexican who had been born just before North America became a union. His hair was as black as his skin was dark, and his penchant for biosuits kept his look at the edge of fashion. He stepped into a shaft of early afternoon light, and his tie's pattern changed.

"It is secure, and has been for about a century," Pavia said with a taint of frustration. He uncrossed his legs, and the sofa complained with a noise that sounded like it could have come from the ass of some enormous beast. Pavia's mass wasn't built from fat. His bulk had been cultivated from a career that included 12 years in Special Forces and eight years of anti-terrorist duty with the NSA. As he waited for the file to appear, the muscles of his jaw worked under a skin speckled by the scars of childhood acne.

Goya leaned onto his desk and lit a cigarette. He exhaled smoke just as the holochive appeared in the center of the room.

"Shade, level four," he said. The room obeyed, dimming the window's glass into dark gray panels that blurred the cityscape beyond. His smoke spread lazily through the data stream, and it rippled slightly.

Pavia leaned forward and intently studied the flow of information as it quivered before him.

Goya drew again from his cigarette a long drag, then let the residual smoke linger about his face. He had built upon his father's empire by leveraging Grupo TVid Azteca's world audience share into the second-most-watched Network on the Net. Having grown the company through shrewd acquisitions, Goya had amassed an empire that would secure him a place in business history.

"Stop!" he said.

The data stream froze.

"What is it?" Pavia asked. "What do you see?"

"I don't know." Goya, his face lined from years of dealing with serious matters, peered at the bits of information.

Pavia rubbed his chin, and his meaty fingers scraped across his afternoon shadow like it was 220-grit sandpaper. "Hell," he said, glancing at his watch, "if you don't know, I certainly won't!" He extracted himself from the sofa, leaving a crater no bioleather could restore.

"Sit down, my friend," Goya said with a tone of authority his head of security had come to respect.

Pavia sat, and his pant legs hiked to expose the fur-covered trunks that were his calves. He scoffed as he settled back into the sofa.

Goya continued studying a certain area of the file. "See this?" he finally said, pointing.

Pavia focused on the section.

"Why would she need this?"

Pavia edged between two chairs to get closer to the holochive, leaned in and read.

"I couldn't say," he said, straightening.

Goya crushed out his cigarette. "Look at the download path."

Pavia reviewed the data again.

"Why would a five-year employee – one who has an exemplary record – move this kind of data in such a convoluted manner?"

Pavia thrust his hands deep into the pockets of his Trussardi pants and shrugged.

Goya sighed. "She is either harmlessly retrieving it for some kind of research ..." He eyed Pavia in a way that caught the veteran security man off guard. "... or she's retrieving it because someone has paid her to." Goya lit another cigarette.

"But this is useless information. What could anyone do with this?"

"Resume," Goya said, and the holochive began to slowly stream. "Stop. Extract these files here, here, and here." He touched the holochive, and it instantly separated into three separate files. "Isolate and enlarge." The holochive divided again and extracted the data into large info-panels.

Pavia stepped closer and studied them. Suddenly, his mind saw the pattern nestled in the bits of seemingly banal information. He whistled.

"Yes, my friend," Goya said. "When they are separate files, they have no significance. But seen together–"

"They reveal that our model employee isn't so model." Pavia rubbed his chin again and felt the scar from that assignment in Jordan.

"No, she appears not to be, eh? Light, level 10!"

The window's grayness quickly vanished, and the office filled with early New York afternoon sunlight. Goya eased into his chair and propped his vintage kangaroo Noconas on his desk. They had been his father's.

"Do you want me to bring her in?" Pavia asked.

Goya crushed out his cigarette in the large glass bowl. "No," he said after some thought. "I think we'll let her continue. It should be interesting to see where this goes."

"I must advise you, for the record, I think that is unwise. We don't know who she's working for, or what they are trying to do."

"Don't worry, Oscar. You'll figure it out before it goes too far, eh?" Goya ejected the file. "Here, take this." He flicked it at Pavia.

The tiny wafer sailed through the air; Pavia lumbered and caught it with cupped hands. He grunted from the effort and straightened. "Who is she, anyway?" he asked, pocketing the file.

Goya glanced at his Netport. "Moriarty ... Deja Moriarty. She's in Entertainment."

Pavia turned to leave.

"Oh, and one other thing." Goya folded his hands behind his head. "The more I think about it, the more I feel this one should be off the grid. Agreed?"

Pavia pondered the request. "*De acuerdo,*" he replied in

the best Mexican accent his New Jersey heritage would allow.

"*Bueno*," Goya said, and snapped his Netport shut.

Paris

"**YOU** goin' to hang upside down all morning?" Deja asked from the cocoon she had created with the bed's thermo-blanket.

Chaco relaxed and let his arms dangle. He looked at her. "No," he said. "One more and I'm done." A drop of sweat fell from his forehead and hit the cement floor with a delicate "thap." It vanished into the puddle that had been forming under him for 20 minutes. He grunted and pulled himself up for the 50th time.

Deja stretched and watched her lover hang from one of

the loft's ceiling supports. She often thought how unfair it was that Chaco's muscle tone was more the blessing of genetics than of any structured lifting. What workout he did consisted of the occasional 50 reverse pulls and some new yoga he had been into since before they met. All she knew was that it involved chrome balls the size of melons and required a Liquid Fiber connection to the Net. But what got to her wasn't the fact that it was taught remotely from somewhere in India by a hot female instructor who had thighs that could crush coconuts. It was more that Chaco just had to disappear to the class twice a week. He referred to it as "me" time. "Suspicious" is what Deja called it.

She pulled her knees in and tightened her cocoon. "Doesn't that make you sick, hanging like that?"

"Not really. You get used to it after a while. Throw me that towel, will you?"

Deja flung it in kind of a blind, reverse-flick. It missed his outstretched hands and landed on Chaco's cat. The big tabby growled from under the towel, then scooted blindly across the floor, pawing and jabbing, until it slammed into one of the concrete columns.

"Oh, shit, Meatball!" Deja said.

Chaco twisted to get a better look at the heap crumpled at the base of the column. The cat's exposed tail twitched angrily.

"Don't worry, he's all right. He does that all the time, don't ya Meat?"

The cat's tail flicked and curled as if in answer. Then Meatball popped his head out and bolted across the loft in a kind of crazy sideways gallop.

"See? He's fine." Chaco disengaged the boots and lowered to the floor. "He'll probably have a headache for the rest of the morning, but that's a cat's life, isn't it?" Deja groaned and pulled the blanket over her head. Chaco fell onto the bed and began playfully grabbing at where he thought her waist might be. She squealed and thrashed at his repeated jabs.

"Jesssus, Sonny!" Deja sat up and pulled the blanket off her head. She caught her reflection in the floor mirror and saw her product-brittle hair was splayed as if a small nocturnal animal had been nesting in it.

Chaco retreated from his attack to the edge of the bed and looked her over. "Nice style, baby."

Deja smiled and answered with her middle finger.

"So elegant this early in the morning." As Chaco left the bed, he passed his hand over the tips of her spiked hair, and Deja swatted him away. He walked into the kitchen, and its lights slowly greeted him. Deja fell back onto the pillows.

"About last night," Chaco said. "That was incredible. What got into you?"

Deja opened her eyes to the cobwebs that were building in the rigging of the loft's trusses and smiled. Meatball hopped onto her chest and began kneading. A large drop of drool fell from the cat's mouth and spread into the threads of her T-shirt. She stroked his back, and Meatball purred with appreciation.

"I don't know," she said.

Chaco looked up from pouring orange juice into a large glass and smiled.

Something fluttered across Deja's heart, and for the first time in their relationship, she felt a defined sense of comfort. From the beginning, she had innately sensed a connection with Chaco, and even though he never mentioned it, she was sure he felt it, too. But now, snuggled in the familiar comfort of his bed and barely descended from a passionate ledge that only two people in love could reach, she decided to allow herself the sole emotion she knew little about.

"Hey," Chaco said, filling a second glass. "Are you happy?"

"Yes," she replied warmly.

He entered the bedroom. "Aha! In bed with another man."

"Guilty as charged." Deja gently pulled Meatball's tail as he jumped from her chest onto the shelf behind her. "And this guy never bitches about cold feet. Do you?" The cat playfully sparred with her from the protection of his high ground.

"He's a good guy, as cats go." Chaco settled onto the bed and handed her a glass. He paused and took her in.

"What? Is it my hair?"

"No, baby, it's not."

Chaco took a small sip from his glass, set it on the nightstand, leaned over, and tenderly kissed her. "You know," he said softly, "I felt something last night."

Deja wrapped an arm around his neck. "Me too," she whispered, and leaned in to kiss him.

"Agent Chaco."

Deja stopped in mid-kiss.

"Agent Chaco-san," the voice said again.

"Crap," Chaco said against her lips.

Yoichi Tsukahara's pudgy figure formed in the center of the loft.

"Good morning, Agent Chaco," he said, with a slight bow. His eyes moved to Deja; she pulled the blanket around herself.

"Tsuka," Chaco said, shifting to face the holoimage. "This better be damn good!"

Tsukahara bowed again, more deeply this time. "I'm so sorry to disturb you, but there's been a—"

"Listen, if the drives for the NetLinks are acting up again, get one of the techs to check them."

"No, it's not the NetLink Hubs. They're running at 100 percent efficiency."

"If it's the Data Transfer Units, Davis can fix them. We saw him last night at a party down in the Lower-"

"No, Chaco-san!" Tsukahara's face was grave, and his bow was much slower this time.

"Yeah?" Chaco said cautiously. The holoimage rippled slightly, and its linear waves of pixels oscillated into little moiré ovals.

Tsukahara finished his bow. "Protocol demands you return to the unit."

"Why?"

"This is not a secure channel-"

"Damn it, Tsuka. What the hell is going on?"

Tsukahara hesitantly opened his Netpad and nodded to himself. He looked up. "We believe there has been an accident."

"What level?"

"Ten."

"Shit," Chaco said under his breath.

Deja looked from her lover to the holoimage and back. "What, Sonny? What does he mean?"

Chaco turned slowly, his brow furrowed.

"Sonny?"

"Ten is biothermonuclear."

Deja gasped.

"Yeah," Chaco said, "just like Hawaii."

When the Biolution arrived, it swept away many industries that were once the anchors of modern life, and in so doing, changed the dynamics of the world order. The technology it spawned created new sources of synthetic fuels and reduced the Middle East to the status it enjoyed prior to the development of the internal combustion engine. This drove radicals within the Middle East to show the infidels one last act of Arab anger.

On a beautiful spring day in the Hawaiian Islands, the terrorist detonation of an untested biothermonuclear weapon caused the tropical paradise to debiolize, or what TVid pundits aptly labeled "merged." At precisely noon, one million Hawaiians, tourists and military personnel (not to mention all animal, plant and aquatic life within a 300-mile radius) merged like an ice cream sundae on a hot afternoon. There was no flash of light, no rain of fire – just a congealing of matter that shocked the world. What had once been a concept was now a brutal reality whose specter hovered at the rim of the world's collective nervous consciousness like a low-grade fever.

Chaco slowly rose from the bed.

"Sonny," Deja said, "your legs, they're shaking."

"Probably from the workout." He turned to the holoimage. "Disengage this connection."

Tsukahara bowed, and his image disappeared.

Chaco collected his clothes and began walking toward the bathroom.

"Sonny?"

Chaco stopped, but didn't turn. "Yeah?"

"Talk to me. What's going on?"

"Deja, a level 10 could mean anything from a containment

leak to a ..."

Deja could only think that his mind was struggling to wrap itself around the enormity of the situation.

"I better get going," he said, and hurried into the bathroom on the other side of the loft.

Deja sat in the middle of the bed as the morning sun exploded over the top of the city and flooded the loft with hot yellow light. She gathered the blanket around her and began to rock. Moments before, she had been delighting in her newfound ardor, but now, all had changed. Meatball hopped from the headboard and nestled into the crux of her legs. He looked up and purred. Deja gathered the cat into her arms and nuzzled his face into her neck. The cat licked the tip of her chin.

"Oh, Meat," she said. The cat blinked sleepily. "You're so lucky."

Deja took in the loft, and her attention stopped on a small lip of shelf cantilevered from a wall. It held about a dozen holophotos and hung there, glowing, as a collection of moments that was Sonny Chaco's life: the day he graduated from the Academy, his mother and father's 40th anniversary, the birthday party when he turned 30, and he and Deja on their trip to France. She stared at the holoprint from Paris for several minutes, lost in memory.

Chaco emerged from the bathroom and hurriedly walked across the loft to the dining table. He yanked his coat from the back of a chair and slipped it on in a move that always reminded

Deja of a dance step she had learned in high school. He removed his Netpad and pointed it towards the desk by the front door. A drawer slid open.

Deja hated what was inside.

Chaco walked to the desk and pulled his Light-Force from the drawer. After inspecting its safety, he slipped the weapon into its holster under his coat. He straightened and adjusted the cuffs of his shirt, walked to the front door, reached for its handle, and paused.

"I don't know when I'll be back," he said so quietly Deja could barely hear him. He finally turned. "Feed Meatball, will you?"

Still holding the cat to her chest, Deja nodded.

Chaco forced a smile, then carefully turned the handle and stepped from the loft. The echo of the door clicking shut rebounded off the hard surfaces.

Empty the soul

MARL is haunted by shadows that move through the landscapes of his dreams. Crowds in nameless streets, chanting and screaming, their colorful features twisted into shapes that resemble masks from the largest city on the planet.

Waking, he finds that he is drenched in a sweat that could only come from fear of failure. He opens his eyes to a black void and listens. The hum is still there.

A need to scream rises deep from his being, but he refuses

to succumb. He wipes the sweat from his face and stares at his hands. In the blackness they seem detached, foreign. He turns them over and strains to find their form.

Then it strikes.

The overwhelming sense of a million souls – screaming to him over a threshold that he has come to understand as his gift. Something has happened on the planet, or might have happened. He never quite knows, but its presence is dense and catastrophic.

The accompanying pain slams into his essence with all the force of the universe. He fights the urge to wretch and slowly climbs out of the bed. The tile floor coldly welcomes his feet.

Moving through the darkness, he cautiously inches his way to the bathroom. Its light greets him with the brilliance of a sun, and he collapses onto the lip of the sink. Water automatically flows, and he cups his hands and splashes his face, hoping he can wash away the visions. They begin to recede.

Upon leaving the bathroom, the light fades and plunges him back into the shadows. As he climbs onto the bed, he knows that when he closes his eyes he will see the faces again. They will greet him on the plane of his dreams and ask him why. He does not have the answer. It is not his reason – his purpose – to exist. He has been trained only to stop the madness. He fights for the strength that seems to elude him. He is scared, like a child in a war bigger than he can fathom; he does not see or understand the complexities that shape his future.

Then, with a sudden and desperate realization, he accepts that he must return to his dreams and face the many who are gone. Only then will he know what to do.

He closes his eyes and empties his soul.

You did all right

YOICHI Tsukahara was the latest in a series of "Exchange Agents" the NSA had paraded through Echelon unit over the last year. He was young and talented but still uncomfortable with New American culture. He jumped to his feet and bowed as Chaco entered the room.

"Cool it, Tsuka, you're in the big New 'A' now. We don't show respect here – for anybody." Chaco threw his coat against an available chair and settled against the counter of Tsukahara's

Netport station. He accepted a cup of coffee from Cooper.

"Morning," Davis said, engrossed with something on his Netport screen.

"Hey, boss." Steiner busily consumed the last of a crusty apple Danish. The other techs didn't even look up.

Chaco studied each one of his console-jocks and tried to get a read on their emotional states. "So, what do we got?"

Davis turned and stretched. "One hell of a headache," he said yawning.

Chaco kicked his legs out from under him, and Davis almost toppled backwards. "We have a Mag 10 in system, and you're bitching about a hangover?"

"We do?" Steiner said, spitting Danish past Chaco's legs.

All the techs turned to their Netports and began clutching at their VirtGear. Davis struggled to his knees and tried jacking into the system.

"Wait, wait, *wait* a second!" Chaco said, pissed. "I came down here on my day off because of a Mag 10 alert!" He turned toward Tsukahara, who was slowly recoiling from a deep, apologetic bow.

"I am so sorry, Agent Chaco. I misread the alert."

"Well, what the hell is it? Are we under an alert or not?"

"Yeah, boss," Steiner said, wiping his mouth. "Technically, we are."

"But it is not a Magnitude 10," Tsukahara said. "It is a

magnitude one *point* zero."

Everyone in the cramped lab restrained their laughter.

"Give me your Netpad," Chaco said.

Tsukahara sheepishly offered his Netpad and flinched when Chaco grabbed it.

"Jesus, Tsuka, the organics in this pad are almost dead. Get over to the Cage and requisition a new one." He threw the Netpad, and Tsukahara clumsily tried to clutch it before it clattered to the floor.

"Hands like a fish." Chaco relaxed against the counter and rubbed his face. "Any more surprises this morning?"

"Negative on that," Davis said, righting his chair.

Chaco sighed, knowing that what could have been an excellent day with Deja was now going to be another "issue." It wasn't like he didn't want to be with Deja. It's just that working for the NSA meant you basically were 24-7. It was a small price to pay for national security. Or was it? He sniffed at his cup. "Who made the coffee this morning?"

Everyone looked at Tsukahara.

Chaco shot a look at his intern. "Not your day, is it?"

Tsukahara nervously grinned. "Ah, no, Chaco-san. It's not."

"Agent Chaco?"

"Yes, sir?" Chaco asked as the image of his superior appeared on the console's screen.

"Please stop by my office when you get a moment."

"Yes, sir," Chaco replied, knowing that, with Slowinski, "when you get a moment" meant right now.

"Trouble, boss?" Steiner asked.

Chaco shrugged. "Not that I can think of." He began to leave but got only as far as the door. "Hey, what was the mag one about, anyway?"

Davis searched through some online files at his Netport. "Looks like a biopharm lab outside of Paris had a loss of pressure in their resonance chamber."

"Can you isolate it?"

Davis slipped on his VirtGear, and its optic couplings wrapped around his head like the tentacles of some deep ocean crustacean. They hissed as they searched for their contact points. For a moment he looked about, riding the wave of data back to its source. "Got it!" he declared. "Looks like a biotech firm. Let's see, my French is a little rusty, but I thinks it's pronounced *La Société...commerciale des...MarionNettes de Viande?*"

"Okay," Chaco said. "I think I caught some of that."

"*La Société commerciale des MarionNettes de Viande,*" Tsukahara said in perfect French. "Literally translated: The Meat Puppet Corporation."

"What was it? Can you tell?"

Davis paused. "Yeah, kind of. It's all in French and ... Latin? That's weird. Anyway, it was a small accident, and yeah, just as I thought, right in the resonance chamber. Hmmm, that's interesting."

"What is?"

"This data doesn't look like your typical corporate tech."

"Cloning?"

"Possibly."

"That's not a mag one. Alert ops. Do they have it contained?"

"Yeah. Seven injured, no deaths. It'll probably hit the French news in a half hour. Be on the majors later today. Nothing special as far as I can tell."

Davis jumped to his feet and began grabbing wildly at his VirtGear. He knocked his chair across the room. "Jesus H. Christ!" he screamed and stumbled into his console. "Get this goddamned thing out of my head! Shit!" Davis clenched his teeth in a seizure-like lockdown, and his body froze in a contorted spasm.

Some of the techs started to approach.

"Don't touch him!" Chaco yelled, and the techs stood their ground.

"Man, what the hell hit him?" Steiner asked.

"I'm not sure." Chaco stepped closer and inspected Davis. "It looks like something backwashed into his VirtGear's Network, but the security walls should have stopped that."

"Predator stream," Tsukahara said, referencing his console.

Chaco looked at Tsukahara and frowned. "If you got a clue, I want to hear it."

Tsukahara glanced again at his console. "Russian made,

very dirty." He looked up and wiped sweat from his upper lip. "I've studied this extensively at the University. If he's not released within two minutes, the stream will begin to restructure his nucleotide polymorphisms, and any other deoxyribonucleic acid sequence variants."

"In English."

"It will make him a vegetable."

"Okay." Chaco turned to the group. "Anybody got any ideas?"

Tsukahara stepped over to the emergency shut-off button on the far wall and lifted its plastic cover.

"Wait a second!" Steiner said. "He's totally Virt-In. You can't auto-down on him. That's for fires and shit. It'll kill all the power to this grid, and probably him with it." He looked at Chaco. "Won't it?"

Davis was beginning to take on the appearance of a freakish modern sculpture. He was slowly vibrating like an electrical surge oscillated in him, and foam was building at the corners of his mouth.

"Hell if I know," Chaco said. "This isn't in any of my background. Tsuka, do you know what you're doing?"

Tsukahara studied the room. "Russian Predator Stream is very black-ops. It can't be stopped. It operates like a virus, and just keeps adapting."

"Shit," Chaco said under his breath.

Tsukahara hit the button; the room went black.

Being a "clean" room – which had always struck Chaco as such an odd holdover since rooms didn't really need to be sterile anymore – buried 10 levels below the Maryland landscape meant that when the power was cut, it got, as his grandfather used to say, as black as the Ace of Spades.

"Everyone all right?" Chaco asked into the darkness.

There were grumbles in various degrees of "yes."

Steiner clicked on a miniature flashlight and directed the beam to where Davis had collapsed. As the light passed over Davis' VirtGear, it caught the edges of some disconnected fiber optics, and rainbow arcs danced across the room. Steiner moved it over the rest of Davis's body, which had fallen forward in a sick-looking heap. One of his arms was contorted to one side, while the other had been caught awkwardly under his chest. A small puddle of drool and blood was slowly spreading from his partially opened mouth.

Steiner lifted the light, reflecting it off the ceiling like a spot so the others could see. They rolled Davis over, and Chaco pulled out his Netpad and passed it the length of the body. The glow from its tiny screen cast Davis in a steely blue tint.

"What's it read?" Steiner asked.

"He's alive, but his breathing is shallow. His pulse is a little slow, and his blood pressure is off, but not too bad. Except for some broken teeth, I'd say he's pretty lucky." He clicked off the

Netpad and placed it on the counter. "Nice job, Tsuka," he said into the blackness. Steiner swung the light to the wall where the shut-off button was, and all heads followed. Its narrow beam cut a path through the dark, like a spotlight in one of the old prison vids Chaco had enjoyed watching with his father.

Steiner swung the beam around and caught the edge of Tsukahara's face.

"Is he going to be okay?" Tsukahara asked.

But before Davis could respond, Chaco's Netpad hummed.

"This is Security Station 4. Your unit is off-line. Fire crews are headed your way."

"Cancel that, security!" Chacko said. "No fire, repeat, no fire. We have a medical emergency, Category 5."

"Affirmative. Do you want power restored?"

"No! We have a man who's still Virt-In."

"Affirmative. Holding power restoration until we hear further. ETA for med team is three minutes."

There came a pounding at the entrance door that made everyone jump. It sounded to Chaco more like a SWAT battering ram, the kind they used on a TVid show he'd seen once – what was it called, *Cop for a Day?*

Steiner swung the light toward the noise, and Chaco stepped toward the door, but something caught his foot and sent him stumbling. There was more pounding.

"Agent Chaco?" Slowinski beckoned from Chaco's Netpad.

"Jesus." Chaco stepped back and followed Steiner's beam back to the counter.

"Your 'situation' has come to my attention."

"Yes, sir, Mr. Slowinski. You see, we had this Russian Predator thing–"

"Agent?"

"Yes, sir?"

There was a slight pause that Chaco took as his boss preparing to unleash his own special brand of disciplinary action. "See me when your *situation* is under control."

"Yes, sir." Chaco wiped his forehead with the back of his sleeve and leaned against the counter. He looked down at Cooper, who, along with another tech, was trying to extract Davis's VirtGear. "Be careful of the optic couplings," he said. "They usually carry a little residual juice."

The pounding at the lab door stopped.

Steiner handed the flashlight to another tech and began helping the others delicately uncouple the dozen tentacles that entwined Davis' head. This would have been a simple task in any other situation, but because Davis was still connected to the Net, they had to uncouple the connectors in the correct order, or his nervous system could go into shock.

Harrison read aloud from his Netpad how to release the connectors. When Steiner removed the last one, its living properties sensed freedom and recoiled into the main housing at the front of the headgear.

"There," he said with an air of accomplishment. "That's the last one." Steiner lifted the VirtGear from Davis's head with the reverence of a surgeon. Davis's head rolled out of the housing, his cheek stopping just shy of the pool of blood and drool. He eyes were half open and partially rolled back. His jaw had unclenched, but his nose looked broken. Chaco's Netpad hummed again.

"This is the med team. We're standing by outside. Is your victim still Virt-In?"

"Negative," Chaco said. "Bring us back online."

The overheads, along with the lab's equipment, emitted a collective drone, and Chaco and the others shaded their eyes from the harsh light. The door to the lab hissed, and the med team rushed in and quickly surrounded Davis.

"Hey, Yoichi," Steiner said. "You okay there?"

Tsukahara glanced toward Davis, who was being raised on a med platform to be hovered out. "Will he die?" he asked.

"He's going to be okay, Tsuka…. Isn't he?" Chaco asked of the lead med tech, whose name patch labeled him as Morrison.

"His vitals are stable, and he'll probably eat with a straw for the next two weeks. We'll know more after we get him into Scanning. What did you say that stream was called?" He signaled his team to begin moving Davis out.

"Russian Predator," Chaco said.

Morrison frowned. "I haven't seen anything like that in a

long time. Wonder why the Walls didn't stop it?"

"Hell if I know. I thought they could stop anything."

"They're supposed to. You better run a diagnostic on your Virt Hubs before I have to come back down here and haul out another one of your fried asses."

Morrison scanned the room. His attention landed on Steiner's collection of antique cell phones. "You Net agents are an odd bunch."

Chaco shrugged.

"What do you boys do down here, anyway?"

"Just keepin' the peace."

"Peace, my ass." Morrison followed his team out. "I'll let you know about your agent here, as soon as I know something," he said over his shoulder. The door shut behind him with a clunk.

The room filled with a tense energy as Chaco, Tsukahara, and the techs all stood silently collecting themselves. Chaco edged the tip of his boot into the puddle of drool and blood. "Somebody want to clean this up?"

"Way ahead of you, sir," Cooper said, making his way forward from his desk. He slipped on some latex gloves and began attacking the puddle with a bottle of the bio agent that turned body fluids into dry putty that could be scraped up.

Tsukahara stepped up as Cooper spayed the stuff across the puddle. Chaco could tell the scene disturbed him.

"Don't sweat it, Tsuka. You did good."

"Agent Davis could have died." Tsukahara said, still watching Cooper.

Chaco put his hand on Tsukahara's shoulder. "He would have definitely died, if you hadn't acted. You did the right thing, and that's all that matters."

Cool

SINCE her day off had been blown by one of Chaco's dumbass interns, Deja decided to grab a commuter jump jet back to New York City. The world had never been in danger, and Chaco had apologized profusely, even buying her an expensive dinner at U-Topia before her flight. But Deja wanted to get ahead of the week's business, and besides, Chaco hadn't seemed all that insistent on her staying the weekend, anyway. All in all, she at least got a great night of sex and a good meal, which unfortunately summed up their relationship at times. Not that that was bad, but she knew she had felt something the other night that had vaguely presented itself as love – and she just wanted to know if Chaco had felt it, too.

Deja played with the volume of the vid screen in the seat in front of her. She moved up and down the range, but the sound didn't change. It was loud enough to irritate, yet not enough that people would turn and stare. Resigned to the fact that she was powerless to control the only real luxury afforded to passengers these days, Deja went back to staring out her window. It was weird, she thought, watching the ground shrink as they ascended into the late Maryland evening, that she was traveling on an airline called Southwest in the Northeast. But after the airline industry collapse earlier in the century, which facilitated Southwest's purchase of American and United, she figured they were big enough to call themselves whatever they wanted.

One of the holo attendants cleared its throat, an odd act, considering it had neither esophagus nor anything to clear. Deja figured it was the result of programmers who couldn't think of a better way to get a passenger's attention.

"Would you like anything to drink?" it said too politely.

Deja peeled herself from the window. "Yes, please. I'll take a vodka tonic."

"Thank you. That will be 20 Ameros."

Deja handed over her chip card, which the holo attendant

held for a moment to read the encoded information before it returned it and moved on to the next row. A real attendant came up the aisle and passed through the holo image, creating, for a split second, the eerie illusion of two faces merged.

Suddenly, Deja's seat started reclining. Its cushion, which had already reshaped into a basic reading position, began contorting to Sleep Mode by firming itself and creating a small pillow. Deja quickly reset the seat's protocols, and it started to reconfigure. The seat was designed to monitor Deja's vitals, but she wasn't that tired.

A human attendant returned with Deja's drink and set it on her tray table. Deja took a sip and settled back. She started flipping through the channels on her vid screen and landed on an NNN news segment about advanced language chimps being tested by the telemarketing industry in California. The woman next to her stirred and gave out a small moan.

"I'm sorry," Deja said. "The volume on this screen must be stuck." She fiddled with the buttons in her armrest. The woman, who had been facing the aisle, turned. Her catlike eyes dilated in the dim cabin light to reveal bright rings of orange around the pupils.

Deja quickly focused her attention back to NNN, which had segued to a news segment concerning the hazards of bioregeneration for correcting cosmetic issues in preteens, now that it had become all the rage in upper middle-class suburbs. There was a moment of awkwardness, then the woman lightly touched Deja's arm.

"What do you think?" she asked.

Deja hesitated. "Excuse me?" She tried not to stare.

"I asked what you thought of that news piece." The woman gestured at the vid screen, which now displayed a commercial for biodiapers with nanotechnology that actually "ate" the baby's waste. The woman's pupils narrowed, then dilated back to normal. They were beautiful, although Deja sensed a great deal of sorrow behind them.

"Well, ah ... I thought that ..." Deja looked to the vid screen and back. "... it's pretty egotistical of parents to allow their children bioaugmentation at such an early age. It's, well, just silly!" Being unable to think of anything better than "silly," she mentally chastised herself.

The woman considered Deja for a second and burst out with a laugh that seemed to have been trapped for years. "That's precious," she said, covering her mouth as if laughing were wrong. "You're so wonderfully accurate with your assessment. Sir?" She hailed a holo attendant passing up the aisle. "I would love some champagne, and?..." She gestured to Deja.

"Oh, no I–"

"Please." The woman's eyes flared slightly. "I *insist*."

"All right," Deja said, not listening to her better self, which she had been doing a lot lately. "Another vodka tonic, please."

"Splendid," the woman said, holding onto the "s" for an effect Deja couldn't quite understand.

*   *   *

"... so this intern," Deja explained, "screws up the magnitude level, and instead of a 10, it's a really a one – a one point zero!" She squeezed a lemon into her fourth drink, and its spray hit the woman in the eyes. "Oh, jeez, Corazon, I'm so sorry. Um, that won't, ah, you know, damage them, will it?"

The woman, still laughing, took her napkin and dabbed her eyes. "No. Besides ..." She looked over to Deja, who was restraining her laughter. "... I can always get them replaced."

Deja sipped her new drink and wondered about Corazon's eyes. They had an odd quality about them, almost digital. "Can I ask you a personal question?"

Corazon's expression shifted, and Deja sensed she might have stepped over some unspoken boundary. She chastised herself again. "I-I'm sorry, never mind."

The woman's look softened. "That's all right ... I have nothing to hide."

"Okay," Deja said, pressing the crinkled edges of her napkin flat. "How old are you?"

Corazon smiled, as if there was some personal joke at work. She pondered the question while she swirled the champagne in her glass. "That's a hard question to answer, really."

Deja, feeling the effects of four vodka tonics, frowned. "Really, why? Everyone knows when they're born." But she stopped with the sudden realization that Corazon's eyes may not be the only manufactured thing about her.

A smooth and knowing grin spread across Corazon's face. She raised an eyebrow. "Boo," she said softly.

Deja gasped into her drink while Corazon chuckled.

"Are you, you know, one of *those*?"

Corazon leaned over the armrest and into Deja's face. "Yes," she said, evenly. "I'm a 'Silent Human.'" Her irises narrowed until her eyes were almost completely orange.

A cold chill slammed through Deja's vodka buzz. She shuddered and almost spilled her drink. "Neat!" she said, dredging this word up from the same suppressed area of her brain that had offered up "silly."

Corazon's look changed to one of puzzlement, but she laughed. "Well," she said, "I've never had a reaction like that before."

Deja began chuckling too, though she wasn't really comfortable with it. "No, seriously," she whispered before she took a big swig from her drink. "I've always wanted to meet one of your kind."

With this, Corazon's demeanor shifted again, and Deja feared the misplaced harshness of her last statement had caused it. Why did her brain, when it tried to select the right thing to say, and especially when she needed it the most, fail her so consistently? It had gotten her in trouble more times than she could count. To her surprise, however, Corazon seemed unfazed, as if being referenced as a "kind" was perfectly natural. Her expression relaxed, and as Deja studied the clone's manufactured beauty, she finally realized what had been bugging her since the moment they met.

Corazon had absolutely no flaws.

Even though she had probably been made in the image of someone – a dead wife or girlfriend – she was flawless. Her complexion was perfect. Her hair, teeth, lips, even the arc of her neck seemed sculpted to resemble a conglomerate of ideals. She was a perfect product of a DNA regeneration stew that much of the world had banned 20 years earlier.

"So–" Deja began.

"I'm three years old," Corazon said.

"Whoa," Deja said, referencing from the Moriarty phrase file. "That's amazing!"

Corazon grinned and took a sip of champagne. "And my full name is really Kita Corazon, but I still think of myself by my tank name: Corazon 13."

"Why 13?"

"Because there were 12 before me that never made it through maturation. I'm the 13th one. *Voilà*!" she said with a gesture at herself.

"So, who are you? I, I mean, who were you? No, wait, I'm sorry, that didn't come out right either."

Corazon patted Deja's arm. "It's okay, I know what you're driving at. Really, I'm fine with it all." She paused for what Deja took as the clone struggling with her own definition of life. She delicately sipped from her champagne, handling her glass in a way that could have only been cultivated by intense schooling. "What people don't realize is that most of my kind have been brought into fairly wealthy situations. It's just too expensive a proposition for anyone except the super rich to take on. And I'm really very grateful to be Mrs. Alberto Goya. I'm taken care of, and I have most everything anyone would ever want, and - why Deja, you look like you're going to be ill."

Deja felt the blood drain from her face with the realization that Alberto Goya – the same Alberto Goya she had been ratting out to Chaco – was this woman's husband, or owner, or whatever.

"Is your husband the president of TVid Azteca?" she asked.

"Yes."

The guilt punched Deja in the stomach with all the nausea of extremely rancid sushi. The cabin started to spin.

"My dear," Corazon said, "you look terrible. Let me call an attendant."

"No, please. I just need to use the bathroom." Deja began climbing over Corazon. "Excuse me." She hurried down the aisle and bumped into a flight attendant she had mistaken for a holo.

"Easy there, young lady. Do you have to go that bad?" He pushed one of the lavatory doors open. "There you are, all to yourself."

Deja nodded "thank you," stepped into the tiny room, and

proceeded to puke out her guilt, which had been welling up ever since she had started passing the damn info to Chaco over half a year ago.

Deja took a drink of water and tried to gargle away the burning in her throat. The pounding in her head she attributed to the vodka. There was a knock at the lavatory door.

"Are you all right in there?" It was the flight attendant who had let her in.

"Yes," Deja managed.

"May I come in? We have others who need to use this lavatory."

Deja unlocked the door and the attendant poked his head in.

"Have we been over-served?" he asked through a professional smile.

"Possibly," Deja replied in a voice way too husky for her own good.

"Oh, love the voice, dear. I have friends who would kill for that."

Deja gingerly edged up the aisle and settled into the bio comfort of her seat. Sensing her blood alcohol level, its living foam began to cradle her. She looked over to Corazon, who was doing a fairly poor job of restraining her laughter.

"Don't say a damn thing," Deja said.

"Oh, dear, I feel so bad for you."

"You think you feel bad." Deja accepted the blanket Corazon offered and curled into as tight a ball as she could. Its fabric cycled through various shapes, trying to accommodate her.

Corazon reached over and stroked Deja's forehead. "Thank you," Corazon said tenderly.

Deja was startled at Corazon's show of affection. Even though she was bioengineered young, she now appeared older. Not as old as a mother might be – more like a big sister, which was kind of comforting since Deja had grown up an only child of workaholic parents. Besides, she felt like shit, and Corazon's touch was soothing. "For what?" she asked.

"For listening. I don't tell many people the truth. I sensed you're the type who wouldn't pass judgment, and those are rare to find."

Deja smiled as the dehydration and trauma of puking began to take its toll. Her seat started to recline. "Corazon?"

"Yes?" She was still stroking Deja's head.

Deja struggled to keep her eyes open. "Is it weird, you know?..."

"What? To live in the shadow of someone else?"

"Yeah."

Corazon smiled. "My kind have a saying," she whispered. "It's better to have been made for someone than never to have been made at all."

Deja tried to think of something to say, but her seat had

become comfortable, and her mind was too tired to do anything but dip back into her file of sophomoric phrases. "Cool," she finally whispered.

"Sleep well," Corazon said.

The hairy eyeball

THE office of Chaco's director was a study in excruciating efficiency. Every file and Netpad was in its place. The photo of President Alberts hung on the wall with what Chaco took as the politically correct distance between the two other North American Union leaders. Even the Slowinski family holophotos were arranged on the credenza in alphabetical order according to name.

Slowinski burst into his office, barely grazing the trim of the glass door as it automatically read his retinal signature and slid to one side. He moved his wiry frame through the room's austerity with all the grace his lifetime of military service had taught. Chaco thought he heard his heels actually click as he stopped behind his desk.

Slowinski gestured. "Please, sit down."

Chaco sat, keeping his body forward and his back straight. In his first meeting with Slowinski, he had made the mistake of displaying a more relaxed attitude. He often wondered if that's why he had spent his first 18 months in the Decoding Unit.

"How's your situation, agent?" Slowinski asked, settling into his chair.

Chaco had learned never to flinch. Ever. "Under control, sir."

"And your man?" Slowinski asked with a cold stare. Chaco's dad had called this "giving you the hairy eyeball."

"Initial scans show him stable, with no neurological damage. They took him to George Washington. We should know something later today."

"Davis is one tough son-of-a-bitch. You've got nothing to worry about with him, son."

Slowinski was a classic throwback. A lifer. And when he used the word "son," it meant the old man was edging ever so slightly toward his emotional side. He went back to staring at the holoprints of the NAU leaders "Unbelievable," he said finally.

"*Sir*?" Chaco asked.

Slowinski pointed. "I still can't get over it."

"What's that?"

"Hell, I can barely tolerate one female president, but three?"

"The people have spoken."

Slowinski, still eyeing the holoprints, twitched slightly, like he was confirming to himself that his value structure was firmly in place. "How do you feel about your progress with the Goya case?"

"Good, sir."

"And that girl?" Slowinski looked back. "Is she ... *tight?*"

Had Slowinski asked this over a few drinks, Chaco might have mistaken the question, but in this context it meant: was she secure? More specifically – could he trust her?

"Yes, sir," Chaco said, trying not to disclose his new feeling. He and Deja had always gotten on like porn stars, but the other night something had changed in him. It wasn't like an epiphany or revelation, which is how he thought it might feel. Just a shift. And it took him completely by surprise, because Deja was supposed to have been nothing more than a vehicle for information. He never thought that this ditzy girl with a model's body and electric hair would give his heart a wake-up call. The plan had been to engage her, use her, and discard her. Now, however, Chaco found his emotions fighting with his agency training, which was basically wet-wired into his being.

"Here." Slowinski casually picked up a Netpad and flung

it into Chaco's lap.

Chaco spun the pad around and broke its seal.

"We're adding a little bonus material to the Goya case."

Chaco quickly sampled the pad's folders until he came to one that contained conventional black and whites, along with some vids. All the files centered on a man captured in various environments. There were several images from Reagan International, a Lower End convenience store, and Union Station Mall. The man appeared normal, yet seemed to be wearing the same clothes in every image. While Chaco studied them, he noticed a slight shift in the coat's pattern and color.

"What's the bottom line here?" he asked, still reviewing a particularly clear image of a tall woman in the convenience store folder.

"The bottom line is in the meds. Check out file F."

Chaco clicked to the folder and scanned through it. He was pretty adept at reading medical charts, but these didn't seem to make sense. "Are these real?"

"You tell me."

"According to these stats, this guy is ... *180* years old? That can't be right."

"Keep going," Slowinski said. "There's more weird-ass shit in that file than I've seen in my whole career."

Chaco continued through the data, then stopped and read one with more detailed meds. "Jesus," he said to himself.

"Well, he's not that, but from the looks of it, he can't be quite human, either."

Chaco read on. "What is this guy?" he asked finally.

"We don't really know. He just appeared on the grid 40 days ago, like he dropped out of the goddamned sky."

"Maybe he did."

Slowinski engaged the hairy eyeball. "I would keep your focus on terra firma, agent. There're not going to be any damn aliens on my watch, is that clear? Besides, I'm sure our boy here is the good ol' fashioned homegrown variety. But the thing that gets me is the DNA sampling. If he's a clone, then he's something new, because you don't get those kinds of readings and not be black. And if he's not working for us, then he's a threat to national security, *period*." He hit the top of his desk with his finger to punctuate his meaning.

"But, sir, what can my department do? This looks like more of a DoD issue."

"Click back to folder C and scan down to file 14."

Chaco complied and came to more conventionals of the tall woman browsing in the convenience store. She had to be wealthy, considering the coat she was wearing, and then Chaco noticed her eyes. It was hard to make out, but they had a cat-like quality, sort of like Meatball's, but not so golden. And what was with those orange rings? He came to a fuzzy high-angle shot of the store's interior, probably lifted from one of the security cameras. The aisles were crowded, not unusual for the time of night, and to the right of the checkout was the woman. She was making a transaction with the counter guy, an old Asian as far as Chaco could tell. Something caught his attention, and he clicked up the magnification. Standing near the counter was the man again, wearing the same clothes as in all the other images.

"Okay ..." Chaco said hesitantly. "Are they together?"

"Go to the next sub-folder," Slowinski said.

Chaco clicked through more images of the orange-eyed woman on board a commuter flight, similar to those that ran between New York and Washington. She was talking with a female passenger who wore one of those stupid head wraps that were so hot right now. In the sixth image, the orange-eyed woman was laughing and leaning forward enough to fully expose the face of other passenger. At first she didn't register, but it suddenly hit Chaco. He zoomed in on the base of the head-wrapped woman's neck and saw Deja's tiger tattoo. A chill crawled down his spine. He looked up.

Slowinski raised an eyebrow. "The plot thickens."

"Sir," Chaco began, but the word caught in his throat. "Are they all connected in some way?" He thought he came across pretty calm.

"We don't know yet. But when I saw your mark there ... what's her name?"

"Moriarty, sir. Deja-Ann."

"Right. Well, that's when I said to myself it's time for Mr. Chaco to step up to the big leagues. Are you ready for a little field work, agent?"

"Yes, sir."

Slowinski nodded in approval.

"Who is this woman with the weird eyes?

"Her name is Kita Corazon Francesca Goya. She's the wife, or I should say new wife, of Alberto Goya. Are you getting the picture here?"

"She must be a clone, because our sources told us that Goya's wife died over three years ago in an accident. His PR department spinned it that she was having treatment abroad for cancer."

"Affirmative. She's probably one of those Caribbean jobs. I don't like the smell of this, and I'll bet you a week's pay that they're all mixed up together." Slowinski highlighted his last statement by stirring his finger in an imaginary pot.

Chaco doubted seriously that Deja was involved, but there was something very strange – decidedly unnatural – about this guy who never changed clothes. And what the hell was Deja doing getting shitfaced with a silent?

"I want you to leverage whatever you have with this Moriarty girl and build a profile on this clone who seems to have only one suit. He's our wild card, mark my words." Slowinski went back to staring at the presidents.

Chaco started to get up.

"One more thing," Slowinski said.

Chaco teetered, his legs half bent.

"If you're dipping your pen in the ol' Moriarty ink, don't get involved. Do I make myself clear?" He shot Chaco a look that jumped off the hairy eyeball scale.

To mend what?

DEJA stared into her drink and watched the chemical fusion between its fruit juices and alcohol – what the bartender had called a "1-900-FUCK-YOU-UP" – become a hypnotic party in a glass. She didn't have a clue for what the 1-900 meant, but had a good guess for the other part.

"It won't kill you," the bartender said. He laughed, and the gold loops around his neck began humming as they interacted with the rings hanging from his ears. He might have been cute, Deja mused, except for the spiderweb tattoo that had replaced his hair. His laugh became a raspy cough, and his tattoo slithered across his skin and collected into a dark patch on top of his head. "Shit," he muttered between hacks, "I'm gonna need to get regen'd."

Deja watched his tattoo reform as he walked to the end of the bar. This wasn't the first time her best friend had stood her up, but she was beginning to get tired of the cycle: get mad at boyfriend, get back together with boyfriend, tell Deja all about great makeup sex. She sucked down half the FUCK-YOU-UP in a single draw and looked around the bar.

Desperate Sense was the kind of club that gracefully milked its fame like an aging diva. It was named after its owners, the famous German rock band, and had ridden every trendy wave since opening 20 years ago. It was "the" club where New Yorkers could party with the elite of the vanities crowd. But for the last few years, it had maintained a quiet chic, relying on its restaurant for more and more of its business. It had on file a veritable who's who of genetic profiles, and its chefs were very tight-lipped about their more famous patrons' gastronomical fetishes.

The restaurant was out of reach for Deja's line of credit, but the original bar was still relatively affordable – or at least it was for her friend, who usually picked up the tab out of the vague guilt she felt for making Deja listen to her problems. Even if Deja was a little fed up with her friend's trials, there was usually someone famous at the bar she could check out.

"You went through that in a hurry," Damien Torres said, leaning onto the bar. "What's the matter? CeCe stand you up again?" He pointed at Deja's empty glass, and the Bvlgari caught the halogen spotlight. He flashed a set of exquisite teeth that came across almost as one continuous unit.

Deja didn't grace him with an answer; instead, she motioned to the bartender for another round.

"You haven't returned any of my calls." Torres slid the last of his martini's olives off its skewer and began inspecting it.

"I was in DC," Deja said, still trying to attract the bartender's attention.

Torres knocked back his drink in one smooth, cultivated movement, then whispered in Deja's ear, "When are you going to realize that this policeman of yours is a loser?" He eyed himself in the huge mirror that ran the length of the bar and placed the olive between his teeth.

The bartender presented Deja's drink with a nod to Torres. She shifted on her stool and took a long sip. The drink's title was beginning to make sense. "Damien, for one thing, he's a Net Agent, not a police officer. Besides, Net Agents have so much more to work with than lawyers." She glanced at his crotch and took another sip.

Torres smiled coolly around the olive, sucked it in and grabbed Deja's arm. He leaned into her face, chewing. "How would you know? You've never been with a lawyer." His face froze mid-chew as a thumb and finger the size of sausages wrapped around his neck. Torres gave out a pitiful cough and a little chunk of olive flew past Deja's shoulder.

"This asshole bothering you?" the man attached to the hand asked. He was the size of a small truck, yet moved with a surprising grace.

Deja looked from Torres's slowly whitening face to the man. His jaw was grinding away as he waited for her answer.

"Ah, no," she said. "I mean yes. *Yes* he was."

Corazon stepped from behind the man, and her coat changed pattern as she passed through the light from a halogen spot. She patted the rescuer's shoulder and slipped her sunglasses into her purse. "I think you've made your point, Oscar," she said to him.

Torres gasped as the man released his grip. "Yes, Ms. Goya." He looked at Deja. "Are you all right?"

Deja nodded.

Torres tried to protest, but the man glared. Torres sat down and went back to rubbing his neck.

"My dear," Corazon said, gently hugging Deja. "We were just leaving when I saw you at the bar. Then this man grabbed you, and well, I asked Mr. Pavia to intervene. I hope you don't mind."

"No," Deja said.

"May I join you?" Corazon asked.

"Sure," Deja said.

Pavia grabbed Torres by the collar. "Give the lady your seat," he said and lifted him off the stool with the same effortless motion he had displayed before. "You and I need to have a little chat on manners." He looked at Corazon and motioned in the direction of the lobby. "I'll be over there, ma'am." He walked Torres from the bar like a puppet.

"You must forgive Oscar," Corazon said, climbing onto the stool. "His methods are somewhat crude." She glanced at Deja's drink. "What are you having?"

"It's called a 1-900 ..."

"Yes, a 1-900 what?"

Deja shied. "Fuck-You-Up."

Corazon looked down into the swirl of colors. "Really? I *must* try one."

*   *   *

While Deja and Corazon talked, the crowd at the bar ebbed and flowed with the cycles of the late-night New York party scene.

"This boyfriend of yours sounds very intriguing," Corazon said when she finished the last of her sixth 1-900.

Deja watched her lick the edge of the glass. "You've had six to my two, and you're still coherent. That's amazing."

A wicked little grin came over Corazon. "Not really. I've

been genetically predisposed to have a high tolerance for alcohol." She motioned to the bartender for another round for her and Deja. "Alberto likes it that way. Better for entertaining."

"Hey, Cor," Deja said. "See that guy at the end of the bar? I think he's got the hots for you." She nodded toward a man seated to the left of the drink station. He was alone and had a strange presence Deja couldn't define. It was like the world in his immediate space had been cranked down to a slower tempo.

Corazon discreetly glanced over her shoulder, and the man looked away. "Why, I think you're right," she said, turning back.

The bartender placed fresh drinks down. "Compliments of the gentleman." He gave a nod in the direction of the man.

Deja and Corazon raised their drinks to their benefactor, but he had vanished from his stool.

"That's very odd," Corazon said.

"Not in this bar. Believe me, you get all kinds." Deja took a sip.

"Hello."

Deja turned to find the man standing next to Corazon. He was addressing her and acting like Deja didn't exist.

"Excuse me for being so forward, but I wanted to compliment you." His coat was made of the same living properties as Corazon's, and their thread patterns began shifting toward each other.

"Thank you, but for what?" Corazon asked.

"Your eyes."

Deja thought she saw Corazon blush under her genetically perfected skin.

"Why, I'm flattered, Mister?–"

"Just, Marl," he said.

"Well, thank you Marl. It's not every day that I get a compliment from a handsome man."

"That's a shame, because a woman with your beauty should be complimented every day."

Deja watched as Corazon and Marl edged toward each other. Their coats took on a sheen that bordered on radiant. In the glow, Corazon's orange rings revealed their true brilliance.

"What do you like about my eyes?"

Marl's smile taunted Deja, and he had an air about him that was familiar.

He raised his hand slightly, as if to touch Corazon, but hesitated. "They're beautiful."

"Really?" Corazon said, shifting her drink to her other hand.

"Yes," Marl said, "they're excellent workmanship."

Corazon's expression faded, along with her coat's glow. Deja sensed Pavia move through the bar's dense crowd and appear at Marl's side, his jaw in overdrive.

"Is this guy bothering you, Ms.–" But before he could

finish, he froze, his hand poised just above Marl's right shoulder.

Marl's demeanor hadn't wavered. He studied Corazon as she set her drink on the bar and began nervously fishing the sunglasses out of her purse.

"Is this man with you?" he asked, as if this question was the most important one in the world. He gestured to Pavia.

Corazon cautiously looked up. "He is."

"I sense that he would die to protect you."

"Yes, I believe he would."

"Is he your husband?"

"Heavens, no."

"I'm sorry if I offended you."

Corazon and Marl eyed each other for a moment.

"You don't remember me, do you?" he asked.

"No," Corazon said, "I most certainly don't."

"I know you enjoy old movies, like *Casablanca*."

The tension in Corazon's body language fell away. It seemed that this statement hit a nerve in the clone's memory. "You're the man I spoke with ... in that little Korean shop?"

Marl smiled through his Zen-like calm. "I see the bruise has healed."

This observation seemed to move Corazon, but this time Deja saw a profound hurt wash over her.

"Does he hit you often?" Marl asked.

Corazon didn't answer.

Deja, transfixed in the moment's elegance, suddenly noticed that no one in the bar was moving. She glanced to the restaurant and saw that everyone was frozen in place.

"You and I are a lot alike," Marl said.

Corazon looked back. "How's that?" she asked. Their coats began to glow again.

"We were both created for a purpose."

Corazon passed her fingers down Marl's lapel; the coat's pattern surged toward her hand. "I was created to mend a man's heart," she said.

Marl smiled again, and Deja realized that the glow wasn't emanating from his coat, but from him.

"I, too, was created to mend something." Marl's voice had taken on a musical quality, rich in a bass level that was straying into subsonic. He moved closer to Corazon, but Deja never really saw any motion.

"To mend what?" Corazon asked.

Marl raised his hand and traced the line of her jaw with his fingers. "Your world."

Kick his ass

10

THE silence hung heavily in the limousine and was broken only when the vehicle's instruments dialogued with the vast Interway grid of Manhattan Island. Deja stared at the back of Oscar Pavia's head. The car came to an intersection and slowed to a halt.

"Ms. Goya," Pavia said, navigating his mass around the steering toggle. He leaned onto the center console and addressed her through the opening that separated the driver's area from the passenger compartment. "I'm sorry for what happened back there."

Corazon, who had been staring out her window for the last 12 blocks, drew a question mark in the condensation her breath had created. "Tell me, Oscar," she said, tracing the question mark again. "What exactly *did* happen?"

The car pulled forward, and Pavia's attention returned to the road.

"I'm not sure," he said. "He must have been using some kind of neurogenic dampener. If my Netpad had been functioning, it would have recognized the source and possibly neutralized it."

Corazon laughed slightly as she spelled out MARL in a fresh patch of breath. Deja figured she was thinking the same thing about Pavia's statement: pretty doubtful.

They were passing the high-rise residences that lined Central Park, and the silence returned. Deja began to remark about how she never came here much, but stopped and decided that for once she would listen to her better self. She sank against the seat and watched the old buildings rush past in a blur of affluence and fame.

Corazon tapped Deja's arm, snapping her back. "What do you think happened back there?"

"Well ..." But Pavia's head turned slightly, and Deja hesitated.

Corazon entered a code on a panel in her door's armrest, and a divider glass began growing from the edges of the two front seats. Pavia glanced back, his jaw angrily flexing in protest. Deja's ears popped as the glass sealed off their compartment. She cautiously glanced at Pavia, who had been reduced to a globular silhouette by the divider's argon tinting.

"It's all right, dear," Corazon said through a knowing little grin. "He can't hear us."

Deja leaned onto the center armrest. "I don't know, Cor. I've never seen anything like that before."

"Nor have I."

"How did he freeze all those people? I mean, is Mr. Pavia right? As far as I could tell, nobody was moving. Or did I imagine it all?"

"You didn't, dear, because I saw it too."

Deja shook her head. "What's really strange is that one minute Marl was there, the next he was gone ... like that. Did you see him leave?"

"No."

"And why was I able to move when everyone else was frozen in place?"

Corazon leaned onto the center console. "Maybe because he sensed you were a friend."

"Thank you for thinking of me like that. You know, even though we just met, I feel like I've known you a long time."

"To tell you the truth," Corazon said, "you're probably one of the only true friends I have. Except, maybe, for Dr. Haderous."

"Who's that?"

"The lead technician in my development."

Deja paused and took in Corazon's beauty. It wasn't till now that she noticed how elegant the clone's bone structure was. Deja had never met Goya's real wife, so she didn't have any reference to compare the two. Considering all the other "corrections" that Goya had made, she guessed Corazon's features had probably been enhanced.

"Tell me, Deja," Corazon said. "Do you really think he has ... How did you put it? ... 'the hots' for me?"

"Oh, yeah," Deja said. "That was the best come-on I've ever seen."

The car fell into silence again, and Deja and Corazon bounced slightly while its suspension adjusted to the road.

"Hey, Cor. Do you think Marl is a, well, you know ..."

"A Silent One?"

"Right. I mean he had such a strange way about him, don't you think?"

Corazon closed her eyes and smiled. "I thought he was wonderful. And yes." She looked at Deja, and her rings narrowed. "He's a clone, but he's not like me. This man is *very* different."

"Spooky is what I'd call him. But what if he's something else, some kind of ... super-clone?"

"Don't be ridiculous."

"No, really. You'd have his baby, my Network would do a special, and I'd be producer of the year!"

Corazon rolled her eyes and laughed, but a melancholy quickly washed over her, and her attention shifted to the passing cityscape.

"Hey, Cor, I was only kidding.... Cor?"

"Deja," she replied, still staring out the window, "I can never have children. It's another one of my predispositions."

"I'm sorry. I didn't know." Deja took her hand. "Another one of Alberto's requirements?"

Corazon sighed. "Sometimes I wish I could ..." She turned back and took Deja's hands into hers. "Promise me something?"

"Of course. Anything."

"Promise me that if he hurts me again, you'll help me leave him?"

Deja considered her request. "Sure I will."

"Thank you." Corazon kissed Deja on the cheek.

Deja pulled the center console back and put an arm around Corazon. "Don't worry. If he hurts you again, we're going to kick his ass."

As the limousine continued uptown, Deja sensed how delicate Corazon was. It didn't feel like she had the correct mass, and her frame seemed as if her body was held together with high-tension wire. She stroked Corazon's hair, trying to comfort the clone, but having never had a sister or a mother, Deja was afraid her effort was marginal, at best.

The limousine pulled up in front of Deja's building and

stopped. Pavia rapped on the divider, the silhouette of his hand looking even more massive from the refraction.

Corazon tapped in the code, and the divider retreated into the backs of the front seats.

"Your apartment, Miss Moriarty," Pavia said.

The car door slowly opened, and a rush of cool night air cut through Deja's blouse. She collected her coat and began to get out.

Corazon grabbed her arm. "Wait ..."

Deja could tell Corazon was struggling with her new emotion. "It's okay," she said. "Just tell me what you're feeling."

"Do you think I should–" Corazon looked away.

Deja smiled and leaned next to her ear. "Don't worry," she whispered. "I think he's the kind of guy who'll find you."

My dearest mother

"**GOOD** f'ing night!" Cooper pushed away from his station and stood. "Or maybe I should say good morning." He glanced over at Tsukahara. "You okay with taking the late shift again?"

Tsukahara looked up from his Netport. "I can handle it, sir."

"Then I'm heading home." Cooper grabbed his coat off the back of his chair and slipped it on.

"Good night," Tsukahara said and bowed.

Cooper began to reply, but stopped midbow. His brow tightened, then he gave a hollow smile and left the room.

It had been a long week, starting with the "Davis incident" and continuing through four days of intense hub recalibrations. Tsukahara was puzzled by his superior's odd demeanor after his meeting with Director Slowinski. Gone were Agent Chaco's good-natured ribbings, which Tsukahara had come to accept as his superior's unique show of affection. But after the Davis incident and the subsequent meeting with the director, there was a distinct change in Agent Chaco's attitude toward him. The only English word that came to mind was respect. Tsukahara leaned back in his chair and stretched off another brutal day. The clock on his Netport shifted to 2:13 a.m.

All at once, the computers started signaling the detection of a detonation similar to the one in the Davis incident. Panicking, Tsukahara fell forward and slammed into the edge of the counter. He wasn't rated to use New American VirtGear, and hunting through a console could take several minutes. The computers signaled again, and Tsukahara eyed Cooper's headgear. The innocuous disc of biotechnology was no bigger than a slice of sushi roll.

What the hell, he thought. He had already gambled once this week, why not twice?

He pulled the collar of his shirt down, exposed the connector at the base of his neck, and raised Cooper's VirtGear to his forehead. He hesitated, and it quivered in his hands before its tentacles lunged at his face. The cerebral engagement was so strong it snapped his head back. Tsukahara pulled wildly at the unit, but the last tentacle found the connector in his neck, and he succumbed.

As his vision recovered, Tsukahara saw before him the universe known simply as The Net. Anyone not used to the vastness of cyberspace could quickly become disoriented and "crash," but Tsukahara had logged many hours and immediately began searching for the stream that had triggered the alarms. Trying to find the data was like finding a single star in a galaxy. But Tsukahara's training had taught him how to let go of his major senses and listen with his "virtual" sense. He often thought that the West lacked the insight that Eastern cultures took for granted. This innate sensibility was the reason Japan had produced so many Virtual Masters.

Tsukahara released his mind and began sensing for the data stream's "emotional" signature – or as his instructor back at Nippon University called it, its "chi." He quickly recognized the urgent signature and rode it back to its source. The detonation had taken place in the resonance chamber of a processing facility in the West Indies owned by *La Nourriture de la Société Commerciale de Dieux*. It was a Level One, like before, with no fatalities but a larger injury count than the French accident. Twenty-three people had been exposed to high amounts of biohazardous discharge and were being triaged at the scene. A ripple of data caught Tsukahara's attention. At first, it appeared to be a mundane report, but as he studied it, he saw a second message within the data.

Tsukahara began hacking the file into two distinct bundles. While he focused on the task, he felt a tremor run through the Net. Its presence was almost imperceptible, but he had learned never to discount any shift.

Moments like these made Tsukahara feel the most comfortable; floating in the noiseless void of the Net, only his mind and the skill with which he controlled it mattered. He let his virtual sense hunt for the tremor's chi, and within seconds he could feel its energy from somewhere out near the rim of the net. Suddenly, it was all around him. And though he couldn't see it, he could sense it hovering like a panther waiting to strike.

"*Yoichi...*" it whispered inside his mind.

Tsukahara reflexively hacked into a GlobeNet code run, knowing it would resequence when the tremor got within sampling distance. But just before the DC zone, the run ejected him. Tsukahara frantically looked about, but there were no legal data flows to tap. He eyed a 911 stream as the tremor gathered around him.

Screw it, he thought. He punched into the stream and was instantly back in the Washington grid.

Tsukahara pried off the VirtGear and entered the sequence to mask his digital footprints from the DC police. He clicked the load button and watched the code cascade down his screen.

"That was one damn fine ride, mister."

Tsukahara turned and found his superior leaning over his shoulder.

Agent Chaco smiled and motioned to the screen. "Watch your construct variables. The DC cops know our code structures."

Tsukahara spun back and studied his masking. A bead of sweat slid down his ribs.

Chaco leaned down behind his ear. "I love fucking with the DC boys."

Tsukahara shifted perspective to a broader view of the Washington grid. He watched as his masking deflected the DC Police past the NSA's security walls and into the general East Coast corporate zone.

"Nicely done, Tsuka. I didn't know you had it in you."

Tsukahara stood and bowed. "Agent Chaco, I can explain."

"What, that you responded to an alarm, beat a Russian Predator Stream and successfully outmaneuvered some of Washington's finest? Come on, you did better than most of the people in this department. Don't worry. I'm not one of those by-the-book guys. I think there needs to be a little improvising now and then. And by what I saw, you can improvise with the best of them."

Tsukahara wiped some sweat from his forehead and felt the indent left by the unit. "Thank you, Agent Chaco ..." He hesitated.

"You've got more to report?" Chaco asked.

"When I was in, there was ... something."

"Different from the Predator Stream?"

"Yes."

"How's that?"

Tsukahara wiped again. "It was very subtle. Under the threshold."

"Yeah, so? There're lots of things in the Net. Old programming, errant streams, some of that shit's over a hundred years old."

"No, it ... it spoke to me."

Chaco leaned against the counter and eyed him. "It what?"

"Spoke to me virtually."

"What do think it was?"

Tsukahara struggled to find the English word that would adequately describe the presence.

"Take your time. Remember, the bad guys can strike in many ways. If you felt something, I want to know."

"It wasn't evil."

Chaco folded his arms. "Go on."

"I can't find the correct words, Chaco-san."

"Just do your best. Think of a simple word that describes it, you know, like sharp or fast or—"

"God."

Chaco's eyebrows went up. "You felt the presence of God?"

"I can't think of a better word, Chaco-san."

"Ghost in the machine." Chaco said to himself.

"Excuse me?"

"Nothing. So what was god? Male or female?"

Tsukahara hesitated. "Male."

Chaco shook his head and laughed.

"Sir, there is something else. When I was in, I discovered a dual stream at the site of the signal."

Chaco grew serious. "Really? Were you able to feed it back?"

"Just a little. I had to break off when the predator appeared."

Chaco put his hand up. "It's late, Tsuka. Just download it to my pad, and I'll read it tomorrow." He handed Tsukahara his netpad and slipped his coat on. "What did you see when you were extracting that dual stream?"

"Test results from genetic mapping." Tsukahara ported the Netpad and transferred the data.

"Are you sure?"

"Yes, Chaco-san. I'm sure." Tsukahara handed the Netpad back.

Chaco adjusted his coat collar. Tsukahara could tell he was struggling with this new bit of information.

"What do you think?" he asked.

Tsukahara hesitated.

"Just use a single word, you know, like before." Chaco was now studying the new data. "And don't say God."

Tsukahara thought for a moment. More sweat rolled down his ribs. "Cloning," he said finally.

Chaco studied the data for a moment, then slowly chuckled. "I'll tell you, Tsuka, you're just full of surprises. That's pretty much what this data is showing." He looked up. "Well, it's late. I've got an early flight tomorrow. Have one of the guys follow up on this in the morning, okay? Good night."

Tsukahara bowed.

Chaco walked to the exit, but stopped short of the door. "You did well," he said.

Tsukahara watched the door close behind his superior, and the room fell quiet. He pulled his chair up to his station and launched his Netmail.

My dearest mother,
Today you would be proud of me ...

What am I doing?

12

THE questions raised by Deja's dossier had left Chaco with an uneasiness that was fighting hard with his new feelings for her. He just loved the way she laughed, especially when her hair moved like she had used a truckload of static as conditioner. He passed a finger over her file image, and the Netpad's organics quivered.

"What are you up to?" he whispered.

Chaco was finding it hard to wrap his head around this new wrinkle in the Goya case. Every time he started to formulate a plan, his thoughts grew twisted. At first, he thought Deja was distracting him, but then he wrote it off to nerves associated with his first field assignment. Finally, he decided to listen to his gut, which usually served him well, or at least as well as any computer model, and caught the earliest jump jet to New York. He intuited that Deja would be the link between Ms. Goya and the man with one set of clothes, but he had absolutely no inkling where to begin. Maybe if he hung around under the guise of a business trip, he would get to meet Deja's new friend with the weird eyes and, ultimately, the man with one suit.

Chaco sequenced through his itinerary and called up his hotel. On Steiner's advice (because he was from New York and knew all the best places) Chaco had booked a room at The Thin. Steiner assured him that it was very *très chic*.

"Good morning, The Thin Hotel and Spa," said a pretty Asian girl dressed in a uniform from a century he couldn't quite identify. "Where may I direct you?"

"Reservations."

Chaco waited as dancing icons infotained him with the hotel's food and accommodations. Another Asian girl appeared wearing the same uniform.

"Hello, Mr. Sonny Chooko," she chirped, confirming that he was dialoguing with a sim. "Your reservations for one room, queen bed, and full T-Net connection are in system and awaiting your arrival today at 11:30."

She was pretty hot for a string of code. "The name is pronounced Cha-co. And do you have anything with a view and a king?"

"One moment, please."

The dancing icons highlighted the Thin's state-of-the-art fitness center. The spa looked pretty basic.

"You're in luck," the girl said upon her return. "We have a king available with a view."

"Great, I'll take it."

"Excellent. It would be our pleasure to accommodate you, Mr. Sonny Chaco. Please place your right index fingertip in the panel on your screen."

More dancing icons followed, but this time only as a multicolored background behind the security thumbprint panel.

"Thank you. Is there anything else The Thin can do for you, Mr. Sonny–?"

"No, Mr. Sonny Chaco is very happy now."

"And so are we. Thank you for choosing The Thin, New York, a member of the Rim Holdings Co., Ltd. Goodbye."

What was up with that name, Chaco wondered and turned his attention to the ground 28,000 feet below. He didn't care much for flying. The thought of being cooped up inside 50 tons of metal and plastic was unsettling enough, but coupled with being surrounded by business types jacked to their Netpads, the whole experience was a big pain in the ass. Many were virt conferencing, and as Chaco looked back over the rows of passengers, he couldn't help but snicker at all the people with portable VirtGear hugging their faces.

"Would you like anything else?" a holo attendant asked.

"I'm cool," Chaco replied.

"The climate controls are located in your armrest if you're uncomfortable." The attendant moved on to the next passenger.

Looking down at the endless gray mass that blanketed the Northeast always depressed Chaco a little. Even though urban planning had allotted thousands of acres as "green havens," it was still basically a nightmare to live in, unless you were wealthy enough to have a second home somewhere on a beach or in the mountains. And even if you could escape, it could only be for a brief time, because eventually the need to conduct business would drag you back like a bad addiction.

He clicked open his Netpad.

"Good morning, The Thin Hotel and Spa. Where may I direct you?"

"If I wanted a dozen roses sent somewhere today, can you arrange that for me?"

"We would be happy to send a dozen roses, Mr. Sonny Chaco, to anywhere in the world. What is the address?"

Chaco gave the girl Deja's office address, along with a simple note, and settled back into his seat. A dozen coral-colored long stems would set the mood, but only so far. Deja was the kind of girl who could always accept a gift graciously, yet at the same time make you feel she knew there was a hidden agenda, whether there was or not. Chaco also knew that if he could score some tickets to the musical *The Giuliani Story*, the king with a view would seal the deal. He clicked his Netpad open.

"This is Deja."

"What are you doing?"

"Handling another Bishop Green crisis. Where are you?"

"Sixty miles out of La Guardia, preparing to land."

Deja's expression softened. "Oh, really? And what brings my handsome government agent to the Big Apple?"

"Got some business that might keep me here for a few days."

Deja moved closer and filled the screen. "And where are we staying?"

"Midtown, high up."

"With a view?"

Chaco smiled.

"Why, that's funny." She faked a small cough. "I'm feeling a little sick all of sudden."

"Then I'm here at the right time. You're going to need someone to take care of you."

Deja rested her chin on folded hands and revved up that sexy look Chaco loved. "I'm thinking *lots* of bed rest."

"I'll call you when I land."

Deja coughed again, winked, and kissed the screen.

Chaco slowly folded his Netpad shut. "What the fuck am I doing?" he said, which earned him a sideways glance over the top of the *Times* from the suit next to him.

Mr. I've-Always-Got-a-Plan  13

ACCORDING to its marketing site, The Thin earned its name because it looked like it had been force-injected between two skyscrapers. Its history page said it had been a sweatshop a couple of centuries ago, but today, it was one of New York's premiere hotels – "a vertical sanctuary of five-star elegance." Only one side had windows, and the really great views were above the 12th floor. The rooms were styled like a designer had thrown-up her entire portfolio, but at least the linens were nice, especially the pillow Deja had tucked under her chest. It was practically as big as her and firm enough to be a major threat in any serious pillow fight.

The room's air conditioning sent a cool breeze across Deja's back, which felt good since only moments before she had been sprawled on the window sill, reeling from probably the best orgasm she had ever had. She peered through the room's darkness at her lover's naked silhouette. He was by the window with his head pressed against the glass.

"Sonny?" she asked, picking through the cheese and fruit tray that had waited patiently for them from the time they returned from dinner. "What are you thinking?"

"Nothing, really," he said. "Just checking out the city of lights."

"I think that's Paris, lover. New York is the city that never sleeps." She threw a strawberry and hit the middle of his back. He didn't react.

"What's the matter?"

He kept staring at the early evening cityscape.

Deja rolled off the bed, walked to the window, and pressed herself against him. They smelled of sex and sweat, and she treasured the feel of his body against hers. She wrapped her arms around his waist and looked up at him through her bangs.

"Nothing, I'm all right," Chaco said heavily, still watching the endless river of yellow CitiCabs.

Deja put her finger to his chin and guided his head from

the window. She rose up on her toes and kissed him. "Come back to bed," she whispered and stepped away, tugging him along by the hand.

Chaco held his ground and gently pulled her into his arms. "Where are we headed?" he asked softly.

Deja had never seen her lover so serious about them. It was wonderful. It was also a little scary. "I don't know about our future," she said, "but I do know that for the first time in my life, I'm happy. And that's usually something I'm not very comfortable with."

Chaco smiled down at her.

She tenderly began kissing his nipples and could feel him grow excited against her thigh. "Come on, lover, the night's young." She stepped away and tugged at him again.

This time Chaco gave in and followed her to the bed. He nestled himself between her legs and began kissing her breasts.

Deja tenderly cradled his head. "Make love to me, Sonny," she whispered, then wrapped her legs around him and accepted him with all of her heart.

*   *   *

The waitress's nameplate was hanging on for dear life. It dangled from a rather interesting sweater whose living fabric depicted the last seconds of the band *Kryptic Kill* before their tour plane slammed into oblivion on a Colorado hillside. The plane, with the heads of the four band members popping out of the windows like balloons, arched across her partly cloudy chest and exploded into a mountain that materialized with chilling realism over her right breast. Afterward, the whole thing dissolved into the words "Born to Die." The logo was perfectly rendered in chrome and hung in the partly cloudiness as if it were somehow profound, then slowly vanished. Had the sweater been programmed for music, it probably would have faded into a guitar lick that could rip an eardrum. The handwritten nameplate pegged the waitress as "Gives-a-Crap," which seemed to Deja to fit.

"What'll it be?" asked Gives-a-Crap as the plane exploded.

"What's good?" Chaco replied.

"Nothing."

"I'll take two eggs scrambled and some toast."

"And you?" she asked Deja, the band now once again approaching their destiny with the mountaintop.

Deja studied the big faux blackboard behind the front counter. "I'll take a protein shake and two honey ecobars."

"Figures," Gives-a-Crap said while the boys went up in flames. She headed for the counter, and the back of her sweater animated the band's image morphing with the "Born to Die" logo.

"You come here often?" Chaco asked. He sipped his coffee and grimaced.

"Only when I want to be alone," Deja said. "This place has character."

"It's got that." Chaco glanced around the Bar of Soap's eclectic mix of washing machines, dryers, Netport stations, and cafe. An old concept, but one that still worked in New York since retrofitting an apartment could set a person back years, and doing laundry had always been a traditional way for people just to get out.

"Here you go, babes." Gives-a-Crap set Deja's shake down, and some its contents washed over the sides in a lather of green ooze. She motioned to Chaco. "Don't like your coffee?"

"It's okay, just a little bitter."

"Here, try this." Gives-a-Crap took a thin, rectangular bottle of golden liquid out of her apron's pouch and poured a generous portion into Chaco's cup. "Now it's hazelnut." She slipped the bottle back and walked away.

Chaco tentatively took a sip. "It's better," he said, surprised, and leaned back into the booth.

"Tell me again why you're in the city?" Deja asked, attacking her shake.

"Doing some field work on a new case. Profiling the financials on a capital investment group. They might have ties with organized crime."

"What happened to the Goya case I was helping you with?"

"Low priority. Things shift fast, and I just go where they

need me. You know I've been wanting field work for some time now."

"And in New York. How convenient." She licked the straw.

The waitress slid the plate of eggs up to Chaco and handed Deja two ecobars. "Here you go, you two lovebirds."

Chaco watched Gives-a-Crap shuffle to another table. "Do you think anyone saw us at the window last night?" He scooped a fork full of eggs that weren't the right shade of yellow.

"Nothing New York hasn't seen before."

"Oh, I don't know about that."

Deja felt Chaco's fingers walk up her inner thigh, and she almost coughed up some shake. She wiped her chin and slapped Chaco across the head with her napkin. "Sonny, now stop that! You know how ticklish I get. Especially after, well, you know." She giggled.

Chaco smiled around another forkful of the suspiciously colored eggs. "So, what's been going on? I didn't hear from you after you left Washington."

"Not much, really. Green is on a ratings tear again, and you know how he gets about them."

"How's CeCe? Is she still as screwed up as ever?"

"Oh, God, yes. Her new boyfriend is such a loser. He actually used her chipcard when she was out of town doing one of those, you know, political things she produces – something for The National Lesbian Firefighters Association. Anyway, he ran up this huge debt."

"When's the last time you made a new friend?" Chaco asked innocuously. He sniffed his second piece of toast, put it back on the plate, and pushed it aside.

Deja shrugged, knowing that if she revealed her friendship with Goya's wife – even if the case had been shifted to low priority – it could put Corazon in jeopardy. "No time," she lied. "I've been too busy." She sucked down the last of her shake.

"You just need to get out more." Chaco began to finish his coffee, but hesitated and set the cup next to his plate. "So what do you say we take in a play while I'm here?"

"That would be great! Oh, wait, I think I can score us some tickets to *Fracture Town*."

"I was thinking something a little more on Broadway." Chaco produced two ticket chips to *The Giuliani Story*. "Say, tomorrow night?"

"Oh my God, where did you get those?" Deja said, accepting the tiny wafers. She held them in her cupped hands and watched as their vidgrams played a little snippet from the show's famous third act.

"Let's just say someone owed me a big favor."

"No doubt! These are impossible to get." She watched Giuliani's monologue at the 9/11 memorial; it then shifted to the play's logo, theme music, and ticket information. She handed them back, their vidgrams looping, and leaned on the table. "Why do I think you've got this all mapped out?"

Chaco wiped up a little spot of egg with his finger and mashed it into a fine paste. "Oh, yeah," he said, his attention firmly on his fingers, "that's me. Mr. I've-Always-Got-a-Plan."

To protect and serve  14

THE St. James was one of the oldest working theaters on the Great White Way. It and the Helen Hayes were the only two musical houses left that hadn't converted to *HoloShow* technology. Others had switched because of escalating production budgets, driven ever higher by union costs, not to mention unruly celebrities, which the world had raised to such a status that leveraging their star power usually cost as much as an entire production. Besides, what self-respecting megastar would be caught dead in some cramped theater playing to real people night after night?

Deja had told Chaco to meet her in the lobby because her boss wanted her to finish something before he left on one of his European PR junkets. Chaco had worn his best suit – the one with the fibers that moved in sync with his steps – and as he walked through the crowded lobby, he got the sense that a few people were giving him the once-over. Since most of them were women, he didn't mind too much. He was studying the people when someone from behind tapped him on the shoulder.

"Hey, sexy."

Chaco turned and found Deja standing there like she had stepped out of a Vogue spread. Her hair, which usually was in a whacked-out spike-do, had been styled into an elegant wave. A pair of five-inch heels lifted her up to his face, and they were the perfect platform for a silky black cocktail dress that made her look more beautiful than Chaco had ever seen her. The fabric's sheen made her brown skin even darker, like rich chocolate wrapped in black foil. She was – to use one of his father's phrases – "gorgeous on a stick."

"Damn, woman, let me look at you." He took her hand and spun her around.

"Your girl cleans up pretty well, doesn't she?"

Deja wrapped her arms around him, and her perfume filled his being. The room seemed to slide away – leaving him embraced with this stunning creature for whom he was definitely falling.

"God, you're beautiful," Chaco said, oblivious to the rush of people around them.

"Thank you," she replied.

Chaco kissed her, and the lobby lights dimmed.

*   *   *

"I just love traditional theater, don't you?" Deja asked as they stepped into the lobby.

Chaco hardly heard Deja's question. His mind was back in the theater. Like an old scar, the events of 9/11 – even in the post-Hawaii years – still conjured up an intense sense of loss. The end of the play, with its gripping reenactment of the tragedy, almost brought Chaco to tears. He hadn't been even remotely close to that emotion since the death of his mother.

"Something wrong?" she asked, stopping him in the middle of the lobby.

"No.... Well, it's just that the ending ..." He felt that same emotion rise again.

Deja squeezed his hand. "That really got to you, didn't it?"

"Yeah," Chaco said and instantly forced back the emotion. "Come on, let's go get a drink somewhere." He took Deja by the waist and edged into the flow of people shuffling toward the front exits.

Just as they reached them, a large, heavy-set man emerged from the crowd like a barge from an ice flow. His attention was firmly on Deja.

"Miss Moriarty?" he asked, removing his black fedora.

Deja turned. "Mr. Pavia!"

"Ms. Goya was wondering if you would join her for drinks."
He motioned to a woman standing near a side wall. Chaco
recognized her from his case file. She was wearing a pair of custom
micropore sunglasses, the kind the super-rich wore when they
wanted to make a statement. These glasses screamed: Don't fuck
with me.

"Oh, I don't know," Deja said. "I don't want to impose."

"Come on, Dej," Chaco urged. "We were just about to go
have a drink anyway." He gave her waist a little squeeze.

"Are you sure, Sonny?"

"Absolutely." Chaco moved his attention to Pavia. He
extended his hand. "I'm Sonny Chaco."

Pavia eyed Chaco's hand warily for a split second, then
engulfed it in his own. Chaco could feel the ridges of tiny scars across
the surface of his palm. Pavia forced a smile that showed just a
hint of gold at the edges of his teeth.

"And you are?..." Chaco asked.

"Oscar Pavia."

"Mr. Pavia," Deja said, "is Corazon's – Ms. Goya's – ah,
say, what is your title?"

"Her assistant. Please, our car is in the alley." He motioned
to the side exit and moved into the crowd.

Chaco took Deja by the waist. "I thought you said you hadn't met any new friends," he whispered into her ear.

"I just met her," Deja whispered back, "and she knows about you. But she doesn't know about the case."

"Don't worry, I'm off duty. Besides, I'm not working that case anymore."

"Good, because she's my friend."

Chaco pinched Deja's waist, and she flinched.

Pavia glanced back.

"I'll be a good boy," Chaco said, grinning.

"You'd better." She playfully kissed his ear.

The sun-glassed woman opened her arms as they approached. Deja broke from Chaco's grip and hugged her.

"Deja, you look breathtaking." She held Deja's hands and admired her.

"Thank you, Cor."

"And this must be Sonny. Deja has told me all about you."

Chaco shook her hand. "Oh, I'm sure she has," he said, shooting Deja a glance.

"Please, this way," Pavia said, and with one hand he opened the massive exit door like it was cardboard.

*   *   *

"So, Sonny," Corazon said, arranging her coat on the back

of her chair, "I read somewhere that the NSA has a department that monitors worldwide communications, especially the Internet. I believe it's called Echelon?" She scooted closer to the cramped table and tried to get some distance between herself and the press of people. The bar at Merge was beautifully designed, but what it had in style was eroded by its lack of square footage.

"Well, Ms. Goya–"

"Please, call me Cor." She winked at Deja.

"All right, Cor. Even if this so-called department did exist, I couldn't tell you anything about it."

Corazon grinned. "Then tell me, what does a government agent do in this modern age of biotech wonders?"

"I'm a Net operative, or as we're called inside the NSA, console-jocks. We build profiles and hunt down data that can be used against an individual or company, or even a country. But in my unit, we're mostly working against organized crime like the Mafia."

"How about in Mexico?"

"Sure, *La Ema* is one of our targets."

"What about corporations?"

"Yes, but only if that corporation has ties to organized crime, or if they're doing clandestine operations that would warrant federal attention."

"And what do you do with this information?"

"Pass it on to a field team in the form of a brief. Or it can be entered into a case and used by our lawyers."

"Fascinating. Mr. Pavia was also in your line of work. Am I correct, Oscar, that you worked at the NSA?"

A cold chill went down Chaco's spine. He locked eyes with Pavia, who was sitting at the edge of the table's light. They stared at each other for a second.

Corazon laughed slightly. "You must forgive Mr. Pavia. He is a man of action, not words." She raised her drink. "I propose a toast."

"To what?" Deja asked.

Corazon thought for a moment. "To new friends."

They all raised their glasses and toasted, but as Corazon began to drink, a large man stumbled into the back of her chair.

"Fucking excuse the shit out of me," he said, obviously drunk. The pattern in his coat reverbed between two shades of blue.

Corazon looked up. The man's demeanor hardened, and he leaned down and studied her. His drink sloshed over of his glass, and Pavia shifted forward in his chair.

Two other men, equally large and trashed, stumbled up to either side of the first drunk. One of them had a small tattoo of a bull behind his right ear – the mark of a mid-level enforcer in the El Toro crime family. They all wore suits popular with made guys: just pricey enough to fit into a good place, but poorly detailed. Chaco had profiled dozens of guys like this, and their look always labeled them as one thing: losers.

The first drunk slapped one of the other drunks on the

shoulder and pointed at the back of Corazon. "Boys," he declared in a slurred New Jersey accent, "looks like we might have ourselves a silent one here."

Corazon nervously began fishing through her purse.

Chaco and Pavia slowly rose in sync, their hands loose at their sides. Pavia shot a sideways glance, and his look was all business.

The first drunk leaned down behind Corazon's ear. "Whose little whore are you?"

In the low light, Chaco could see Pavia's eyes moving carefully about. His ex-agent instincts were probably assessing factors like the size of each man, the distance to strike, the exits, the reach threshold, and the potential of lethal force. The guy's jaw was grinding away.

Corazon slipped on her sunglasses and hunched slightly in anticipation of what was coming. The first drunk straightened and hesitated for a moment, as if he were summoning all his bigoted courage.

"I hate fakes," he said. "Especially the bitches."

The word fakes, like "nigger" a century earlier, cut through the silence that had enveloped the table. But before the first drunk could finish the "s" in bitches, Pavia moved with such speed it caught Chaco off guard. He grabbed the guy closest to him with his left hand, while his right dove inside the guy's coat, probably after whatever weapon resided there. The guy let out a gurgling sound as Pavia's hand closed around his windpipe.

The first drunk, startled by Pavia's actions, stumbled backwards over a four-top of club girls. One screamed, while the others jumped out of the way. The table flipped, sending ice from a Champagne bucket spraying into the crowd around the bar. Before Chaco could move on the drunk with the tattoo, he had pulled out a knife and was holding it against Corazon's temple. The knife was a German organic one only available on the Black Net. Chaco knew from his classes that it was surgical grade and didn't show up on older scanners. If they got though this, he'd find the club's owner and drag his ass in.

The club girl's scream brought the whole bar to a standstill and shifted Pavia's attention to the knife at his boss's wife's head.

Chaco froze halfway around the table. He knew from his training that the look on the knife guy indicated he was riding on Jack, probably right at his apex.

"Let's all fucking stand down!" the tattoo guy said, his eyes wild. He shot a look at Pavia. "Let go of Hector!"

Pavia released his grip and slowly took a step back. He glanced at Chaco.

"Now," the tattoo guy continued, "we're going to exit this establishment in a real natural manner, okay?" His eyes darted between Chaco and Pavia. "And we'll take the fake here as a little insurance that you boys won't try anything stupid."

Pavia looked at Chaco and raised an eyebrow. For a second,

Chaco didn't get it, but then it hit him: Pavia was going to distract this asshole, so Chaco could make his move. Then Pavia, who hadn't said a word all evening, screamed a guttural, primal sound, like he was about to tear the tattoo guy's head off. This move triggered other screams about the club, which distracted the tattoo guy just long enough for Chaco to draw his Light-Force.

"Drop the damn knife!" Chaco yelled, as he leveled his weapon. The gun's automatic holo projection hung in the air 5 feet to the side of Chaco. It displayed to anyone who cared to read it his name and agency ID. It moved in sync with the weapon, passing across people at the bar and turning their faces monochromatic shades of green. Its loading sequence's high-pitched whine cut through the silent club; some people gasped.

The tattoo guy's eyes locked on the Light-Force. "Well, what do we have here? A government agent coming to the rescue of a fake?" His voice had risen to a pitch that made Chaco nervous. He was pressing the knife just shy of drawing blood.

"We don't have anything here," Chaco said, trying to recall his training from his hostage class. "Let's all be calm, and we can work this out."

Chaco glanced at Pavia, who was taking another step back. He figured the veteran agent had already sized up his position as being too close to what was jokingly referred to at the academy as the "splatter pattern." Even if just a little matter of a person shot with a Light-Force got on you, it would continue its debiolizing right up your arm or leg, or wherever it landed. All agents had seen the vid on that process.

The tattoo guy eyed the holobadge. "So, Agent Chaco, are you really going to shoot me inside a crowded bar at such close range?... Could get a little *nasty*."

Nasty wasn't the word for it, Chaco thought. More like horrific. The Light-Force was a powerful and highly accurate weapon. Its risk assessment features could calibrate the matter disruption level and automatically minimize the "splatter" effect. But discharging it in a crowded environment was still a risky proposition.

"Well, agent, what's it going to be?" The tattoo guy's forehead was slick with sweat.

Chaco had to act fast; a person cresting could do almost anything, especially if cornered. He glanced to Pavia for help, but Pavia was regarding him with a strange expression, like he was thinking: it's your fucking show, so get on with it.

Chaco cocked his wrist back, like he was going to set the Light-Force down. "I'm not going to shoot you," he said, and then fired straight up.

A woman's scream almost drowned out the cracking sound of the Light-Force. When Chaco's vision adjusted, he saw most of the patrons close to their table rubbing their eyes from the blast's intensity. Pavia had pulled Corazon away and stepped in front of her for protection. The only person not reeling from the discharge was the tattoo guy. He was hunched over and staggering around in a small circle as superheated liquefied aluminum, which a moment before had been part of a low-hanging chandelier, slowly cooled over his head and back. It looked like he had been partially snared by a net of mercury.

"Jesus *fucking* Christ!" he yelled.

Pavia took a wine bucket off a table and dumped its water all over the tattoo guy. The aluminum hissed, and the guy screamed. Then Pavia landed a punch to his chin that made even Chaco wince. The bastard crumpled like his skeletal system had suddenly disappeared.

Chaco leveled the Light-Force on Hector, and Pavia grabbed him by the collar. He dragged him over to where the other drunk had knocked himself out flipping over the club girl's table.

"Here, use this." Chaco reached under his coat and threw him his cuffs.

Pavia caught them and immediately pulled the wrists of the two drunks together and activated the restraint. Like a VirtGear unit, it tentacled around their wrists and tightened until their skin turned red.

"Deja, are you okay?" Chaco said, looking around.

Deja sheepishly emerged from under the table, her hair in its more familiar tangle of spikes and curls. "I'm okay."

She rushed to Corazon and began helping her peel little

drops of aluminum off of her coat. It was a miracle Corazon hadn't been injured.

The people in the bar, like any good New York crowd, had seen it all and slowly returned to whatever they had been doing. The music came up, and Chaco walked over to the tattoo guy, who was now curled on the floor acting like he was seeing more than stars. Finally, two of the bar's rent-a-cops stepped out of the crowd and approached. They looked all of 21.

Chaco knelt. "Those burns look like they going to scar."

"Fuck you," the tattoo guy replied, through a haze of Jack and booze.

"You need any help, agent?" the taller rent-a-cop asked, his voice squeaky.

Chaco looked up. "He's all yours."

"But, sir, aren't you going to file—"

"I said," Chaco stood and leaned into the kid's face, "he's all *yours*."

"Yes, sir!"

"Is something like this also part of your job?" Corazon asked, adjusting her coat around her shoulders.

Chaco grinned. "Yes, ma'am," he said in his best cop voice. "We're here to protect and serve."

Deja came up to his side. "Are you all right?"

"Yeah, I'm fine." He looked to Pavia, who was helping the shorter rent-a-cop peel some of the cooled metal off the tattoo guy. "Thanks, Mr. Pavia, your, ah, distraction did the trick."

"Always has," he said. He ripped a rather long sliver out of the guy's hair. Most of the metal had landed on the guy's back, but a little had dripped onto his scalp and neck.

"Tell me, Sonny," Corazon said. "How is it that you're able to function so close to the flash? I'm still seeing spots, and I'm wearing sunglasses. You act like it didn't even affect you."

"Third eyelid," Pavia said. He helped the shorter rent-a-cop lift the tattoo guy to his feet. The kid cuffed him and shoved him through the dance crowd.

"You're augmented?" Corazon asked Chaco.

"We all are, Ms. Goya," Pavia said, walking up. He pointed to the side of Chaco's left eye. "It's called an ocular nictitating membrane. It's like a cat's third eyelid, and covers the cornea in an event of a Light-Force discharge. If we fired our weapons without it, we'd be blind by the end of our first year." Pavia's eyes went white as if to prove the point.

Chaco laughed under his breath.

"Eww!" Deja exclaimed. "Sonny, you never told me you were augmented."

Chaco engaged his ONMs.

"Stop that!"

"Would it have mattered?" he asked, his eyes green again.

Deja folded her arms.

"I've got a suggestion," Chaco said to the group. "I know

a great little bar on the Upper East Side. I don't know about you, but I could use a drink."

"If you don't mind," Corazon said, "I'd like to go home. This night has been trying. We'll drop you at your hotel."

Pavia took Corazon's arm and did his barge thing through the bar, although the parting of the people was probably more due to the fact that they wanted to give the government cowboy a wide berth. Chaco had his arm around Deja, and he could sense her apprehension as they followed behind.

"What's bothering you?" he asked into her ear.

"Nothing, it's just ..."

"What, that I'm slightly enhanced?"

"No, it's more that you didn't tell me."

"Look, it's not like we go around broadcasting something like that. Besides, it's confidential. Like I said before, would it have mattered if you had known when we first went out?"

"No, of course not. I knew about your connector."

"Okay, then. Let's not talk about it anymore."

They walked in silence behind Corazon, but Chaco could still sense Deja's edginess.

"Come on," he whispered, "it's not like I lied. There're some things about my job I just can't tell you."

Deja was still edgy.

"Look," he said, stopping them in the middle of the dance floor.

She didn't look up.

"I care for you very much, and if you knew everything, it could make it dangerous ... for you."

Deja wrapped her arms around his neck. "That's all I wanted to hear," she said, and a wicked little grin grew across her face.

Landscape of dreams

15

THE maid has accepted the fact that the man in Room 360 never sleeps. She doesn't bother anymore to make the bed or replace unused towels. She only knows of the guest's presence by the water decanter, which she refills before each vacuuming. Today, she inspects the tumblers and finds them untouched. She carefully returns the last glass to its original position on the tray, takes in the room's disuse, and wonders.

*   *   *

Marl lies atop the bed as he has every night. His fingers feel for the blanket's thread count. Knowing that when he closes his eyes he will be haunted by the visions, he sucks in a long, comforting breath and exhales his fear. Will the emotions surface again?

Am I designed to feel?

In the dark, a band of light – probably from a police gunship – glides across the ceiling. His armpits are soaked. Sweat slides down his ribs.

Another breath, and he prepares for his travels. Tonight will be different, though. He will not confront his visions. Rather, he will range across the landscape of dreams to the home of those brilliant orange rings.

Riding the wave  16

CORAZON looked down at the bits of Earl Gray adrift on the caramel skin of her tea. She liked a splash of milk along with a rich spoonful of honey because it made the bitterness more tolerable. But that wasn't how she was supposed to take her tea; she had been designed to prefer one lump of sugar in Darjeeling, not Earl Gray. Dr. Haderous had called it a glitch in her cognitive mapping.

Once, early in her first year, she had overheard Alberto talking to Dr. Haderous. There had been something foreboding in

Alberto's voice, especially when he said, "Let's rethink her condition." But after the call, his attitude toward the glitches changed, and he seemed resigned to topics like "How to Drink Tea."

Corazon set the cup on the nightstand and crawled into bed, which to her felt more like climbing. The bed had been one of Kita Goya's designs, and its mass was a dominant force in the calculated architecture. The room's temperature was set for 65 degrees – something about the cool nights at one of Alberto's old vacation homes in *Real de Catorce*. While this usually let Alberto sleep soundly, it always left Corazon shivering.

Glitch in the mapping.

Alberto was gone on business, and Corazon had their New York apartment to herself. She pulled the comforter around her and set its temperature control for 75 degrees, then picked up the virtbook she had intended to start for the last three weeks. It was entitled *A Conversation with Your Inner Child*. She slid the interface pad out of the reader unit and raised the tiny disc to her forehead.

"This is absurd," Corazon whispered. What was the point of talking with her inner child when she had never been one? What she really needed was a book entitled *Conversations with the Dead Person You Replaced*. Even though she had studied Kita Goya at great length, she would never really understand her ... or her "inner child." Corazon sighed and threw the reader unit to the foot of the bed. Her eyes grew heavy.

Three years ago, Corazon awoke to the faces of Dr. Haderous and his team. Even though they were pleasant and caring, it was a strange sensation to spring into consciousness as an adult. No growing up. No adolescence. Just opening her eyes to existence. Of course, it wasn't like she had woken with a blank slate. Many of Kita Goya's medical problems, such as her allergies and alcoholism, had been corrected, along with potential problems like her genetic predisposition to breast cancer. They also built into Corazon some of Kita Goya's more fundamental personality constructs, like her Catholicism. It had been mapped so perfectly that Corazon always had a vague guilt lingering near the threshold of her morals.

The real achievement, however, was what Dr. Haderous antiseptically termed *cushioning*. It involved re-implanting certain memories, which was a difficult and controversial procedure, even within the illegal industry of cloning. Nevertheless, it helped Corazon with the harsh impact of beginning life at age 34. The memories weren't intended to cause her to wake as Kita Goya, but they did give her a little nudge to start. And Corazon was most grateful to have been spared Kita's last memory of drunkenly falling into the pool, especially when her head struck the coping.

An arc of cold cut through Corazon, and she pulled the comforter over her shoulders. Nestling against the pillows, she let her mind drift and wondered what it might have been like to awaken as Kita. She often wished that Dr. Haderous' team had done this instead. Life would be so much cleaner. She rolled over and knocked the reader unit onto the floor.

Maybe she should be reading about multiple personalities, she mused.

Or maybe she should just go to sleep. And dream.

*   *   *

Corazon awoke to a slight gust of cold air brushing her face. Through the dark, the walls appeared to be translucent: their surfaces rippling in a fluid arpeggio of color and pattern. Even the bed seemed frail beneath her body. Suddenly, a figure coalesced from the shadows. It was a man.

Corazon wanted to scream, but the fear that would have driven this had slipped away. The man walked around the bed and came to her side.

"Hello, Corazon," he said, his lips barely moving and not quite in sync with the words. There was dim light around him that had no defined point of emanation.

"Hello, Marl," Corazon said.

He smiled.

"Am I dreaming?" she asked.

"In a sense."

Marl moved onto the bed, and she slid back to sit against the headboard. He was wearing the same coat she had seen him in at the bar. Its pattern undulated like the wallpaper.

"Why are you here?" she asked, surprised at her calmness.

He hesitated, raised his hand, and let his fingers follow the edge of her face. He delicately separated errant strands of hair. "To understand," he said.

"What do you need to know?"

"What I'm feeling."

"What are you feeling?"

Marl frowned, as if the question itself pained him. "I'm not sure yet, but I know it's important."

Corazon took his hand. His skin felt like warm glass. She thought the light around him brightened. "Why are you here?"

He leaned close. "You're in me, and I need to know why."

She studied the lines of his face. He wasn't really handsome; he was something more, something ... graceful. Behind his eyes, she sensed a depth of understanding that seemed limitless. And it frightened her.

"Don't be afraid," he said intuitively and gently squeezed her fingers.

Corazon let go and took his face into her hands. "I think I know what you're feeling," she said, and impulsively kissed him. The sensation felt like more like drinking, and it sent a wave of pure emotion crashing against her heart.

Marl took her into his arms.

After a moment, Corazon gently pulled away and searched

his eyes for the soul that might reside there. "You were right," she said. "In the bar ... when I first met you."

His brow furrowed questioningly.

Corazon smiled. "You and I are very much alike," she whispered, then pressed her lips to his and rode the wave into the night.

On his knees

17

IT was almost 2:00 a.m. Tsukahara cautiously eyed the VirtGear unit as it sat on a stack of files he had to read by morning. Its simple form seemed unassuming in the soft light of the desk lamp. He began to reach for it, but recoiled from an emotion that took him by surprise. *Fear* was the English word that came to mind. But Tsukahara's curiosity about the presence was taunting, almost pulling at him. He placed the unit to his forehead, and its interface tentacles entwined around his head. The last one found its home at the base of his neck, and his vision slipped away.

After a millisecond of black, Tsukahara's vision faded in. He had no idea how he would find the presence again, so he planned just to empty his mind and hope for the best. In his daily life, he usually could work this naiveté to his advantage, blaming either language or cultural differences for what his colleagues labeled "misunderstandings." Often, his Western hosts would speak more freely around him, thinking he wasn't getting it and thus saying things they usually guarded more closely. But as he hung motionless in the Net's chaotic vastness, he began to question his motive for seeking out the presence.

He looked down at his body, now represented by its preprogrammed digital avatar, and discovered his shoes were jumping erratically from Velcro-strapped cross-trainers to standard-issue Oxfords. Must be an issue with the system's platform translation protocols, he thought. His focus shifted to the chasm of cyberspace below him, and a vertigo-induced nausea boiled up – what console jocks lovingly referred to as "the virts." Even though he knew that what he was seeing was just a programmer's rendition, nonetheless it was still very intense and real. He quickly began the practice of soft, regulated breathing, and the nausea subsided.

Floating silently among the trillions of data streams, Tsukahara began to concentrate on listening for the chi he had previously encountered. He loved the Net. It was a fluid experience and very comforting. After a time, his thoughts wandered. He

PAUL BLACK

thought about his boyhood home in Nagasaki. He recalled his
family's living room, how his mother had insisted it be completely
traditional.

Suddenly his thoughts manifested, and he found himself
standing at the threshold of their living room.

"Disconnect," he ordered, but the VirtGear didn't respond.

The panic that should have been pouring into Tsukahara's
nerves never came. Instead, he was filled with an overwhelming
sense of peace. He glanced down and saw he was wearing white
socks – the kind he wore as a child, complete with the indentation
from a pair of *zori*. He curled his toes and could feel the rice
straw *tatami* mat through the soft cotton. Glancing about, his
attention settled on his grandfather's *jeonju* chest. He walked
over and opened one of its drawers, wondering if their family
album would be inside. The drawer resisted his first pull, then a
memory flashed of his grandfather showing him the secret to the
drawer's stubbornness. He tried again, this time pulling harder
with the left handle. The drawer acquiesced, and he reverently
lifted out the leather-cased antique and began leafing through
its fatigued pages.

As the generations flipped past, a dog-eared, sepia
photograph caused him to pause. It was an image of his great-,
great-, great-grandfather, who had perished in the atomic blast. His
ancestor looked so proud holding his firstborn as he smiled across
the ages. Tsukahara had been told that, like so many that fateful day,

his ancestor had been entangled in the telephone lines and had died, struggling, on his knees. An odd feeling moved across Tsukahara's heart that he couldn't quite define.

Does it sadden you, Yoichi?

Tsukahara's nerves bristled. He slowly closed the album and turned to the center of the room. The presence was all around him.

Does it sadden you? Its Japanese was perfect and came across like a man's voice in his head.

"What?" Tsukahara replied.

This memory.

"Yes ... yes it does."

Why?

Tsukahara thought for a moment. "Because this is one of my ancestors, and he ..." His throat tightened.

What, Yoichi? Why do you grieve over someone you never knew?

Tsukahara fought back the raw emotion building in him. "I grieve because he died so horribly. They say he died—"

On his knees?

Tsukahara froze. Another cold chill carved his spine. Could the presence read his mind?

Isn't it odd that history is segmented by insignificant points in time when there is only one real division point?

"I'm sorry. I don't understand."

All of man's history can be divided by one point on the linear timeline presently observed.

"What point or date is that?"

August 9, 1945.

The warmth of tears welled in Tsukahara's eyes.

This realization pains you?

"No, not really. I'm just grieving for my ancestor."

Silence.

"Who are you?" Tsukahara asked finally.

That is hard to put into words.

"Are you human, or are you an AI?"

I am as human as you, Yoichi Tsukahara.

"Then how did you know how my ancestor died?"

That is equally difficult to put into words. You could say that I have an ability to understand emotions on a deeper level.

"What are you?"

There was a shift in the presence's chi. Tsukahara tasted a tear that slid onto his lips.

You could say I'm an architect, the presence said with what Tsukahara sensed was an edge of pride.

"An architect ... of what?"

Another shift.

The future.

I'll hunt you down  18

"I miss the rattle!" an old man declared.

Chaco looked up, and the guy locked eyes with him like he'd never let go.

"These goddamn LEV's are too quiet. Miss the old trains. Clickety-clack, clickety-clack. That's what it's supposed to sound like. Not this hum!" He pursed his lips and made a noise that sounded more like a high-speed food processor than the N Line LEV. Dark, ratty dreadlocks spilled down both sides of his derelict face and cast his eyes into shadow. The lighting in the LEV was the bluish-green that seemed to dominate all New York public transit. Chaco quickly shifted his attention up the aisle to a pretty Hispanic girl, obliviously jamming to music only she could hear.

Since he was supposed to be in town on business, Chaco had the day to kill. He decided to take in the Warhol retrospective at the MOMA. This exhibit wasn't of work done by the original artist, but by a clone that had appeared on the art scene about 10 years ago. No one really knew how the DNA had been obtained, but critics all agreed that the clone's art was as good as, if not better than, the original. If it hadn't been for the editors at *Art in America* turning him into a media darling, his fate might have been the same as other clones – death.

While Chaco watched the Hispanic girl jam to the silent beat, he wondered how he was going to reconnect with Goya's wife. With any luck, Deja might run into her again, and if the stars aligned, he also might meet the strange guy with one suit. At least, that was as far as his "plan" went.

The old man, probably fed-up with the lack of attention, shuffled to the next car. Chaco tried to relax, but something was nagging at him. He had felt it back at the station – a kind of pressure to the back of his neck. It was the same feeling he used to get as a rookie console jock when he knew he was being tracked. He couldn't explain it; it was just a hunch, like a sixth sense. He had developed it during his days in the military. All tech ops guys learned to develop their senses, and this one seemed to be particularly strong. Chaco's field tests were off the charts, and his unit buddies used to call him Mr. Sensitive. "Common sense" is what he called it.

He studied the car, searching the faces of the other passengers, but they didn't register anything for him. Still feeling a bit uneasy, he left his seat and entered the car ahead.

It contained twice as many passengers. Many were sitting with their backs to Chaco. As he made his way up the aisle, he couldn't shake the feeling, so he slipped into an empty, backwards 3-across and slid over to the window. He was facing a forward 3-across whose lone occupant – a woman, business type – was deep into a virt conference. She looked up from her call and gave him a perfunctory smile, then laughed at something said in her conversation.

The LEV slowed to a stop, and the businesswoman, still conferencing, collected her things and left along with about half the other passengers. While the car filled with another tide of nameless faces, Chaco referenced the route map. He'd go through four more waves of loading and unloading before reaching the MOMA station.

When the LEV pulled forward on its cushion of supercharged magnetic energy, Chaco's sense of being followed subsided. He turned his attention to the window and watched the blurred shapes of the tunnel flow by. Just then, the doors behind him opened, and a passenger entered. Chaco kept looking out the window as the person settled into the seat that had been previously occupied by the businesswoman. The passenger nudged the tip of Chaco's boot, and he looked over.

"You need to work on your street sense," Pavia said, removing his fedora. He placed it on the open seat next to him.

Out of instinct, Chaco shifted to face Pavia, placed his left arm on the back of the two empty seats next to him and crossed his right leg over his left. This made his profile thinner and positioned him for a potential strike. He casually unbuttoned his coat and let his right hand rest near the opening.

"Looks like Tactical Position number 25," Pavia said, rubbing his chin.

"Forty-seven, actually," Chaco replied. "For the new jump-jets, there's an addendum on confined-space tactics."

Pavia continued to study him, which put Chaco on more of an edge. Even though they had casually bonded at Merge with their agent signals and mutual respect, Chaco knew Pavia was an old dog who, if pushed, wouldn't lose any sleep over introducing a green agent to a few tactics that weren't found in any manuals.

"What do you want?" Chaco asked.

Pavia reached into his coat, and Chaco's hand instinctively went to his Light-Force.

"Not to worry, agent. It's just a Netpad." Pavia slowly removed the device and turned it over in his hands so the screen was facing Chaco. He clicked it on.

Chaco watched in horror as much of the information Deja

had collected over the last six months cascaded down the tiny screen.

"Look familiar?" Pavia asked.

Chaco remained silent and continued to watch the data stream. It ended with a barely audible "beep." Pavia snapped the Netpad shut and returned it to the inside pocket of his coat.

Chaco studied the former operative. "How long were you in service?" he asked, stalling.

"Fifteen years, not counting my stint with DoD."

"Then you understand my job."

"I understand the NSA has changed, somewhat, since my time there. Take you, for instance. In my day, console jocks were relegated to the back office. Their contribution was tertiary. But today, you're in the front line. With this ... this Biolution, the world's a dangerous place." Pavia relaxed somewhat, crossing his legs and casually inspecting his fedora as if it had done something that needed attention. "Yes," he said, "the world is a very dangerous place."

Chaco took a cue from Pavia's demeanor and relaxed against his seat. "It has changed, I'll give you that. But what's that got to do with what you've just showed me?"

Pavia pondered this for a moment, then leaned forward and rested his chin on folded hands. His bulk filled the cramped space, and Chaco suddenly realized that he had been tactically one-upped. Pavia, his brow hulking over his eyes, unveiled a smile whose dental work seemed intentionally third world. Each tooth was tipped with gold.

"My employer," he said, "wants to know if the government has any case against him."

If Chaco divulged their findings, he would relinquish any edge he might have. Besides, what they had so far wasn't enough to prosecute. They knew about Goya's offshore holdings and his association with the illicit Caribbean biotech trade. And his cooking of the books was a pretty standard corporate shuffle. What the NSA had really been after was Goya's ties to *La Ema*, but before Chaco could uncover anything of substance, Slowinski had back-burnered that push for the investigation on the hybrid clone.

Chaco shrugged, truly not knowing what he would say next.

Pavia's brow furrowed, and he leaned in farther. "We wouldn't want to involve *Deja*." There was a threatening tone in Pavia's voice, carried along by a businesslike matter-of-factness.

Chaco had been waiting for him to drop the Deja factor. "To tell you the truth," he said coolly, "I'm not on that case anymore."

Pavia leaned back, and the muscles of his jaw began to twitch.

Chaco motioned Pavia forward, like he about to divulge an important secret. The ex-agent leaned closer; his aftershave smelled of something cheap and very last season.

"Besides," Chaco said, almost whispering, "we don't want

to bring up why you, ah, left the agency ... do we?"

Pavia's nostrils flared, and Chaco suddenly understood the phrase "if looks could kill." Pavia leaned back and folded his arms on his chest. He regarded Chaco with a slight smirk. "I see you've done your homework."

The only thing Chaco had done was get lucky. He had run a backgrounder on Pavia, but it had come up exemplary. Even his buddy in records couldn't find any dirt. All agents had something damaging in their records; it just came with the job. Pavia's file was too good, like someone had cleaned off whatever tarnish it might have worn.

Chaco settled into his seat. "It's always smart to know who you're dealing with."

Pavia nodded. "So, why are you in New York? In town to get a little kitty from a particular producer's assistant?"

Chaco smiled professionally. "Well, I wouldn't refuse it if it was offered. But I'm actually here on a new assignment."

"Can you tell me anything about it?"

Chaco hesitated.

"Come on, Sonny, let an old agent live vicariously. I'm basically just a bodyguard for a rich CEO. I want to hear what my old employer's doing to protect this great nation of ours."

Chaco didn't have a better plan and figured he had Pavia somewhat by the balls, although he didn't know why, yet. Obviously, he and Goya thought the government had more on them than they did, which was just fine. "Aw, what the hell," he said. "Here's the situation. I'm searching for a hybrid clone. His stats are off the charts, and he's friends with my mark and your employer's wife." He searched Pavia for a reaction. "We think he's Triad."

"What does he look like?"

Chaco pulled out his Netpad and brought up an image of Marl. He handed it to Pavia. "This guy is very black ops. I've never seen anything like him. Look at his meds. They're weird as hell."

Pavia studied the image. His demeanor dropped to a level of seriousness that put Chaco's guard up.

"Yeah," he said gravely, nodding. "I've encountered this asshole before."

"I've got to build a profile on him, and my only connection is Deja and Corazon. But I'm not really sure how to flush him out. I can't just hang around and wait for us to bump into him at some bar. What's his deal with Corazon? Are they doing some clone bonding thing?"

"I don't know," Pavia said, still reviewing the data. "The night I met him, he hit the whole place with a neurogenic dampener, and that's all she wrote. Still ..." He rubbed his chin, and the scars on his fingers scraped across his five o'clock shadow.

"Come on, what are you thinking?" Chaco asked. "Do you have an angle on this guy?"

Pavia continued to rub, then handed back the Netpad.

"Possibly," he said and grabbed his fedora. He put it on and adjusted the brim downward across his brow.

"Maybe we could work together on this?" Chaco asked.

Pavia regarded him from under the brim. "What's in it for AztecaNet?"

Chaco hesitated.

"Look, Sonny, you're a bright young man. I'm sure you can use that technical knowledge the NSA spent millions on to make AztecaNet's files, what, disappear?"

"I, ah —"

Pavia leaned forward again and grabbed Chaco's left kneecap with his thumb and forefinger. He dug in behind the patella just enough to send a message. "I'm like a bulldog, Sonny. Fuck me over, and I'll hunt you down. Put me away, and even if I'm a hundred when I get out, I'll come after you when you least expect it."

"You know," Chaco said, not acknowledging the pain shooting up from his knee. "It's funny how those case files can get all corrupt and shit. Happens all the time. It's a real shame."

Pavia let go, and his smile, now revealing to Chaco the full achievement of its gold inlay, was frightening.

11:42 a.m.

DEJA glanced at her watch.

11:41 a.m.

She liked having lunch in the small patch of grass across the street from her building. The city would have once called this a Micropark, but today they were antiseptically labeled Embedded Environmental Refuges. Since the closing of Central Park five years earlier after the release of a nanonerve agent by a radical cell of the Rhodesian People's Liberation Army, the city built hundreds of EERs anywhere it could find enough space to plant some grass and a tree. According to the plan, enough EERs would be built during the park's nine-year detox to approximate its 386 acres. But six years later, Central Park wasn't even close to cleaned up, and there had been only 150 acres of EERs built. Finding personal space with anything approximating grass was now practically impossible.

Deja usually took her lunch early to avoid the crowds, but today it seemed everyone had the same idea. The thought of dodging children, dogs, and the occasional soccer ball wasn't appealing, so she decided to head for her favorite juice bar. Maybe if she bought a compound shake, they'd let her sit and eat her sandwich. Hell, she thought, for as many times as she frequented the place, they should let her sit regardless. She was about two blocks from the juice bar when a pair of absolutely kick-ass pumps in a window display grabbed her attention. Any other day, Deja would have continued on, but with Sonny in town, she thought it might be fun to see the look on his face if she stepped into the bedroom wearing nothing but those shoes.

Deja made her way against the flow and approached the window. Its lone holoquin wore a look of perpetual boredom, dressed in a short, black vinyl coat and matching multi-zippered skirt. The conspicuous protrusion of its nipples triggered a vague memory of a girlfriend who bragged of an ancestor who was the first window designer to insist that her mannequins be anatomically correct. An absurdly controversial act that put the store – Neiman something – into the headlines for days. Now, every time Deja spotted an antique mannequin, it cracked her up to think there had ever been a time when people had been offended by something like that.

She leaned down and inspected the pumps. They were delicate and looked like they had been painted onto the holoquin's feet. "Damn," she said involuntarily, reading their price. She was admiring the skirt when she sensed someone behind her. She tried to find his reflection in the window but couldn't get him in focus, which was odd because she just had her eyes adjusted. When a woman walked past whose reflection was sharp and clear, Deja jerked around and stumbled back against the window. The man's coat shifted pattern, and the holoquin's signal momentarily jumped to static.

"Mr. Marl, you startled me."

"I'm sorry," he said, staring.

"What are you doing here?"

"Would you like to buy those?" He gestured at the shoes.

"What? Oh, no, no, I can't afford–"

"I'm sure your boyfriend would like to see you in them."

That's weird. "Well, sure, yeah. He probably would. How did you know that?"

Marl didn't respond.

Deja waved it off. "Never mind." She started walking in the direction of the juice bar.

Marl kept to her side. "May I walk with you?"

Deja gave him a quick sideways glance. "It's a free country."
The sidewalk was crowded, and she had to keep her attention
forward or risk tripping on the person ahead of her. Marl, on the
other hand, never took his eyes off her yet walked through the crowd
with complete ease. "Mr. Marl–"

"Just, Marl, please."

"Is there something I can help you with?" A tall
businessman caught the edge of Deja's shoulder and knocked her off
stride.

"I need your assistance," he said.

This should be interesting. "Really? With what?"

"It's who, actually."

"Oh," Deja said, grinning. "Is this about Cor?"

"Yes. It's about Corazon." Up to this point, Marl's voice had
been calm, nearly monotone. But Deja discerned something in
the word "Corazon," like his inflection was rimmed with joy.

"Look," she said, shooting him another glance, "I know
you're a clone, and I know Corazon's a clone, but she's a married
woman ... and to a powerful man." She walked to the corner and
pointed at the juice bar across the street. "That's where I'm headed.
You're welcome to join me, but we'll have to make it quick. I've
only got 20 minutes to wolf down a sandwich and shake before I
have to get back."

Marl didn't respond, and as they waited for the light to

change, Deja grew irritated. Her morning had been crazy, and with her taking some time off at the end of the week, she knew her afternoon would be even crazier. Now, she had to deal with this clone-thing sneaking up on her in the middle of the day.

He continued to stare, and Deja had had about enough. "Look," she faced him directly, "I don't know where you're from or what you're about, but in this country, it isn't right to hit on a married woman."

Marl remained silent. His goofy grin was beginning to creep Deja out. The way he studied her raised her guard even more than it was.

She matched his glare, and they had a second of stare-down. "Marl," she said finally, "are you understanding *any* of this?"

He reached for her.

Deja stepped back, and her heel went off the curb. "Shit!" She stumbled out of her shoe, tried to sidestep a large, bright-green puddle, but lost her balance and fell to her hands and knees. The liquid splashed all over her.

"Look out!" a man yelled.

Deja twisted and watched in horror as two tons of public transport skidded toward her. The shriek of the bus's hydraulics and her scream merged somewhere near the tops of the skyscrapers.

Deja opened her eyes to the backs of her hands. Between her fingers she could see the bus three feet in front of her, its registration plate glowing. A crumpled foam cup was suspended in mid-swirl two feet off the pavement, and the sounds of the city, which she usually took for granted, had been replaced by an ominous silence. Her face, the front of her blouse, and some of her hair were soaked. The grit of the street beneath the puddle dug into her knees.

"Deja?" she heard, dreamlike at the periphery of her hearing. She looked over her shoulder.

"Are you hurt?" Marl asked. He was standing at the curb.

Deja straightened and looked at him through wet bangs. Drops of the liquid fell from her body only to stop and hang suspended once they left her. She gasped as another one dripped and froze, adding to the dozen or so that floated like little green bugs just below her face and neck. She batted them away, which caused more to freeze all around her.

"Oh my God!" Deja said. She jumped to her feet. The splashes froze in delicate arcs, making the puddle look like a modern sculpture. She cautiously glanced about and discovered that everything as far as she could see was stopped in place. Cabs, people, birds, blowing trash – even the clouds had quit moving across the sky. There was no wind, or sound, or movement – just a dead and desolate calm. She turned and stared at Marl, who was still standing on the curb with a retarded grin on his face. Then the whole scene crashed down in a realization that threatened to drag her dangerously close to the edge of her sanity. Deja began to shake, and as the bizarreness set in, her legs grew weak.

Marl's coat brightened, and its pattern shifted into a mosaic of color. "Please don't be scared," he said.

"Are you kidding?!" Deja asked. "I almost get killed, you bring the world to a halt, and you're asking me not to be scared? And take that shit-eating grin off your face." Deja brushed back her hair and watched more drops drip and freeze. "Oh, God," she said, swatting. "What the hell have you done?"

Marl stepped from the sidewalk and approached. His coat shifted pattern again. "I haven't done anything."

"What do you call *this*?" She waved her arms.

Marl looked about. "New York," he said, coming around to face her, "hasn't changed."

"Hasn't *changed*?" Deja flapped her blouse in an attempt to dry it. She looked down at herself. "Aw, jeez, I just bought this."

Marl reached over and took one of Deja's hands. "You were going to die."

Deja looked at the bus. The driver, his face aghast, was practically standing on the brakes. "What's going on? What have you done to the city?" Her wits were slowly coming back.

"It's not the city."

"What do you mean?"

"It's us who are different." Marl placed his hands into the pockets of his coat.

Deja looked around again. "I don't understand."

"It's a technology that's hard to explain."

"Try me."

"We are ... in between."

"Between what?"

"Moments," he said just above a whisper.

Deja felt her sanity slipping again.

"Look at your watch," Marl said.

She saw it was still 11:41, but hadn't it been about 30 minutes since she left her building? Deja looked from her watch to the juice bar across the street. "Wait a minute ... I mean ... how the ...?" She fought back a wave of nausea.

Marl touched her shoulder. "It's all right. Here." He walked over to a woman about Deja's build, who had been caught in mid-step. He removed a pullover sweater she was carrying and handed it to Deja. "Put this on."

Deja hesitated, looking from the sweater to the front of her wet blouse.

Marl turned away.

"Yeah, right," she said. "Like anybody's going to notice." *What the hell*, she thought. She was already deep into this nightmare, and taking her blouse off in public was the least of her worries. Deja slipped the sweater on and wriggled it down to her hips. It was a little tight, but it would do. She tied the blouse around her waist and combed her fingers through her sticky hair. "It's okay, you can turn around."

"Walk with me," Marl said, and he started across the street.

"Sure," Deja said, sarcastically. "A walk. Why not?"

Considering she was strolling around pedestrians frozen in time with a clone who had just defied the laws of physics, Deja's fear and panic had somehow given way to inexplicable curiosity. They continued in silence for about a block, edging around frozen people. It reminded Deja of an old wax museum her mom had taken her to when she was a teenager.

"What kind of clone are you?" she finally asked.

"What I am isn't relevant," Marl said. "Why I'm here, is."

"Okay, so why are you here? Which, I guess, means that you're not from here. Are you?"

He didn't respond.

Deja's nerves spiked.

"I'm here," he said, "to align the future."

"I didn't know it needed adjustment."

Marl stopped at a little girl who was perched atop her father's shoulders. She had just licked her ice cream cone, and the scoop was threatening to fall on the dad's head.

"Believe me, Deja. The future needs a great deal of correction." He nudged the scoop back onto the cone.

"So what's this got to do with me?" she asked.

Marl resumed walking, and Deja followed him through a group of Asian tourists who were taking pictures of an old building.

"It's not so much you as it is Corazon," he said.

"Why Cor?"

Marl didn't say anything for about half a block. Deja sensed he was searching for an answer. "There is," he finally said, "an underlying power that runs through all living things. It can be a profound source of strength, and at the same time a great weakness."

"Are you talking about our will power?"

"No, it's more basic than that."

Deja thought for a moment before it hit her. "Love ... You're talking about love, aren't you?"

Marl kept walking in silence.

"But what does that have to do with ... Oh, wait a minute." Deja grabbed Marl's shoulder and stopped him. "Are you in love with Cor?"

His silly grin returned.

"Let's review here," she said. "You're a magical clone, who can set everything straight, who's fallen in love with another clone, and you're telling me — a lowly human — that you're going to adjust the future for God knows what. Have I got all this?"

"I need your help," Marl said.

"What can I do for someone who can do this?" she asked with a wave of her hand.

"I believe my solution lies with Corazon, but she is so ... protected. It's awkward for me to see her."

"Can't you just stop everything and walk up to her, like

you're doing with me?"

"I wish it were that easy. I've taken a great risk to talk with you. You'll just have to trust me. I know she considers you one of her few friends, and I need for you to–"

"Okay, time out," Deja interrupted. "Am I on the Net right now?" She pulled back the lapels of Marl's coat and ran her fingers down their folds. "Where's the camera? They've got new ones now that look like lint."

Marl gently took her shoulders and stopped her. "We're not in a game show. In fact, we're not even on the street."

A ripple of fear shot through Deja, and she shrugged off his hold. "Okay, Marl, or whatever you're called, cut the crap! If we're not here, then where the are we?"

Marl regarded Deja like her father did after she had said something stupid. "You're still at your desk at work." His voice seemed to vibrate inside her chest.

Deja tried to jack out, but nothing happened.

"Don't worry, I'm not here to harm you. Quite the contrary, what I end up doing will change the course of humanity."

Now Deja was pissed. "Why all this?... You know, the bus, the puddle?" She stepped closer. "The ice cream cone?"

"Remember when you were six," Marl said, "and you reached up and put your hand on the hot burner in your parent's kitchen on Walker Street?"

Deja's stomach knotted. "What the–" Her voice caught.

"How did you know about that?"

"You knew it was wrong, but you did it anyway."

"I was just a kid!" Deja edged away from him.

"And your mother lectured you about the stove, but you just had to find out, didn't you?"

Deja's heart was pounding inside her chest. She bumped into a woman and almost knocked a package out of her hands.

"For you to truly grasp the depth of my request, I needed to create a learning situation. You see, Deja, you're the type who has to burn her hand in order to listen."

Deja was beginning to suspect that this creature was dangerously more than just a clone. Her rational self was fighting hard to keep the rest of her from turning and running like hell, even though she knew how easy it was to obtain quirky information, especially these days. But what really frightened her was the fact that she had never told anyone about the incident. She had told her parents that she had burned her palm on a friend's outdoor cooker.

"Deja, please. You have to trust me."

She knew she should run, but there was something about Marl – a benevolence that registered on a spiritual level. Deja also sensed something else in him, like he was just a point of contact for something much bigger.

"Okay," she said, "I'm listening."

Marl took another step toward her, but Deja kept her

distance. He acknowledged her and held his ground. "I would like you to arrange for Corazon to meet me tonight."

"I don't know if I can. Besides, why can't you just talk to her like you are with me?"

"I would. But this," he said, looking at the buildings, "is such an impersonal way to communicate."

"You're not, you know, just BSing me for some kind of pervo thing, are you?"

"If I really wanted to hurt you," Marl said, his voice resonating near the base of her nerves, "you would never know it." He turned to leave.

Deja didn't know if she should be scared or relieved by this last statement. "Hey wait," she said, sensing that their "meeting" was over. "How will I get hold of you?"

Marl glanced back. "Don't worry, I'll find you." The goofy smile was back. "Have a nice lunch."

Deja felt someone tapping her shoulder. She pulled the VirtGear from her forehead.

"I asked if you wanted to grab lunch."

Deja rubbed her eyes and tried to shake off the disorientation.

Tooie Coupland was looming over Deja, her arms folded, lunch bag hanging from one hand. She was on the same level as Deja but assitant-produced a juvenile game show popular with teens.

"You look like you've been at one of those alternate life sites again," she said. "What's Green got you researching?"

"Ah, yeah," Deja said with a bit of a headache. "I am, I mean was, at a site."

"Honey, are you all right?"

Deja forced a smile. "I'm okay. Just a little spacey from jacking out."

"Good, but let's hurry. I want to beat the rush downstairs. It's gorgeous day."

"The rush? What time is it?"

"Now, honey, look for yourself." Tooie leaned in and pointed to Deja's screen. "God, you were in deep. Come on. Grab your stuff, and let's go!" She abruptly turned and headed down the hall.

Deja looked at the time code and shivered.

11:42 a.m.

Welcome to Heaven

20

"**DID** you get any time between your meetings to take in the Warhol exhibit?"

Chaco increased the Netpad's magnification so Deja's face would fill most of the screen. "I did," he said. "It was pretty spectacular, considering he did all of it before nanobots."

"Yeah, I saw a documentary on him once. His stuff has this strange quality to it. I just can't imagine how he created those things without tech."

"We should see it together. I wouldn't mind going through it again." A passenger sat down next to Chaco, and he scooted over to the window seat. "So, where do you want to meet tonight?"

Deja hedged a little. Chaco could tell something was up.

"Sonny," she said, and bit her lip, "I've, ah, got to work tonight."

"Really? How late?"

"Pretty late. It's just that, with Green gone, and taking Thursday and Friday off, I've got to get ahead of these ratings reports. You know how Green is when he comes back from being gone." She grinned, though not very convincingly.

"It's worth it if it means I'll have you for a long weekend. Besides, I've got to prep some files before this meeting tomorrow. I could use the time."

Deja leaned in and smiled. "Thanks, lover. I promise to make it up to you."

"So," Chaco said suggestively, "I'm up for a nice dinner. Maybe some sushi. Got any suggestions?"

"How 'bout Sushi Girl?" Deja offered. "It's got a great bar, and the food is yummy."

She held onto the "u" so that it came across kind of cute. Deja had a way of doing that with certain words, and Chaco had grown fond of it. "Sounds good," he agreed. "And if you can leave any earlier, maybe we can meet for a late drink."

Deja grinned. "That's a date. I'll send you their link."

Chaco watched Sushi Girl's site appear in the corner of his Netpad. Its logotype danced into view, followed by two Asian girls who began hacking away at the letterforms until the logo was reduced to a tray of sushi. The girls presented the tray and greeted him personally. They sounded like the twins from an old Japanese monster movie Tsuka had demanded that Chaco watch in an actual theater. Chaco had laughed his guts out at the retro special effects. There was only one place in D.C. that still had the vintage equipment to project film, and Tsuka was really into that purist crap. "Got it, thanks. I'll call you later."

Deja blew him a kiss and hung up.

Chaco closed his Netpad and listened to the hum of the LEV. He knew Deja's body language pretty well, and there was something odd about it. Just that morning, she had raved about the new Italian place where she was going to take him. Now, however, she was all business, which had come out of nowhere. In fact, last night she'd mentioned finishing the ratings reports.

The LEV began to slow. Chaco glanced at the transit map above one of the exit doors and studied the different routes to Deja's office building. The LEV glided to a halt, and its doors slid open.

"Little Miss Work Ethic," he said before he shuffled out with the rest of the passengers.

*   *   *

"Hey pal, how long we gonna wait here?"

Chaco looked up from his Netpad. "As long as it takes."

The cab driver grunted and went back to viewing the sports section. He tapped the main screen on the vehicle's instrument panel to call up a holoclip from last night's New York Yankees game. The batter cracked a foul into the upper deck, and Chaco could hear the faint roar of the crowd through the half-closed ballistic plexi.

"Jesus, you'd think the Yankees were a farm team." The driver spit another sunflower shell into a foam cup.

Chaco shifted in his seat, and his coat fell open. Out of the corner of his eye, he caught the driver's double take.

The plexi divider slowly began to rise.

"I'm registered," Chaco said, not bothering to look up from the file he was studying. He tapped the Netpad, and his badge's holoimage appeared.

The driver pressed his face against the plexi and read Chaco's ID. "I don't get many fares packin' Light," he said, his voice emanating from a speaker somewhere in the cabin. The plexi lowered. "Especially government agents." He motioned at Chaco's coat. "I collect guns. Can I see it?"

Chaco eyed him and glanced at the crowded sidewalk. "Darken the glass."

The cab's windows went black, and the dome light brightened. Chaco reached into his coat and pulled out his Light-

Force. Its matte black titanium housing seemed to absorb the light. He spun it and handed the butt end to the driver.

The driver whistled. "Man," he said, reverently taking the weapon with both hands. "It's so light!" A serious look crossed his brow. "Say, you're not supposed to part with it, are you?"

Chaco gave him his best cop stare. "Go ahead," he said. "Pull the trigger."

"What the–?"

"I thought you New York cabbies had balls of steel."

The driver shrugged and leveled the gun directly at Chaco's sternum. He held it there for a moment, his hand shaking.

Chaco yawned.

The driver moved his aim to the empty seat and pulled the trigger. The instant it clicked back, a tiny section of the gun's butt disengaged and released a dozen buglike bots, which scurried up the driver's arm.

"Sheeeeit!" the driver exclaimed, dropping the weapon. He brushed wildly at the bots, but they were too agile. They ducked and jumped and continued their charge up his arm.

Chaco picked up the gun and clicked the interface button. The bots stopped and vibrated in place like they were waiting for orders. One had made it to the driver's cheek, and he was eyeing it.

"Get these damn things off me!" he demanded.

Chaco turned the gun on its side and clicked the button again. The bots retreated down the driver's arm, jumped onto

Chaco's palm, and marched into their tiny holding cell in the butt of the weapon.

The driver brushed frantically at his nose. "That wasn't funny, pal."

Chaco suppressed a laugh. "The hell it wasn't," he said, returning the gun to its holster.

"Why didn't it fire?"

"DNA recognition."

"So what would have happened if you hadn't stopped those, those ... What are those?"

Chaco settled back against the seat. "They're part of the gun's Emergency Defense Tactics. They'd paralyze you, collect all your vitals and anything else of interest, and send your info back to the lab. Once they're done with you, they fan out and cover the rest of the crime scene, assuming I was rendered inoperative."

"You mean dead?"

"You can be inoperative and still be alive."

"But what if the gun got picked up again, you know, by somebody else?"

"The bots go after that person, and so on and so on, until they get taken out. The idea is that by that time, enough info has been sent back that the perps are screwed. They're fast little buggers, and they can go for years. We had one hunt down a guy months after the crime. Right up the ductwork and into his girlfriend's apartment. He never knew what hit him."

"Man," the driver said, "that's wild."

"Hey," Chaco said, pointing, "there's our girl!"

Deja emerged from the AztecaNet building and hailed a cab. One immediately pulled out of traffic and drew to the curb. Its door slid open, and she climbed in.

Chaco's driver engaged his cab's systems and pulled into traffic. He hung back just enough to stay in visual range.

"You've done this before?" Chaco asked.

"Plenty. There's always some PI snoopin' on a cheatin' spouse. I get 'em all the time."

They followed Deja's cab uptown, weaving in and out of the rush-hour traffic. Chaco leaned over the lowered plexi and reviewed the vehicle's instrument panel. "What make is this cab?" he asked.

"Ah, this here's one of the new Impala Cores. They grow 'em in old Mexico, then ship 'em all over the place. Real nice, this one is. Got your SATNAV, Interway link-ups, and that new shit in the frame." He snapped his fingers. "What's it called?"

"Programmable matter?"

"Yeah, that's it. They say it's the new deal. Soon, everything's gonna be made with it. Cars, clothes, and check this out, say you're in your house, and the sun's comin' in the window and hittin' ya right in the face. You won't draw the blinds. You'll just ask the house to move the window. *Move* the window." He laughed. "I love that."

"They're pulling over," Chaco said with a slap on the driver's shoulder.

The driver pulled to the curb and parked about five car lengths back. "What's she done that's so bad?" he asked.

"You don't want to know." Chaco handed the driver his chip card.

The driver swiped the card and handed it back, then watched Deja emerge from the cab like some exotic creature. He whistled. "Boy, she's a looker."

It surprised Chaco how hard it was to think of her as just his mark. He had to focus, or his heart would get the best of him. "Tell me about this place she's going into."

The driver pointed. "This here's Club Heaven."

Chaco peered through the cab's windshield at an old converted church. Its steeple was about four stories tall, and a massive, circular stained-glass window dominated its front façade. Two colossal wooden doors that looked like they could have been carved during the Middle Ages loomed above two equally imposing bouncers.

"She must be a member," the driver said, "'cause that's the only way in. If you're not, you can forget about it." He inspected Chaco. "You're definitely not."

Chaco opened his door and stepped out.

The passenger window lowered, and the driver leaned over the seat. "You want me to wait for you?"

"Are you armed?" Chaco asked.

The driver patted his seat meshing. "Got a conventional right under here."

"Yeah, hang around. You never know, right? If I need a ride, I'll call."

The driver nodded and fished an old-fashioned paper business card out of the console between the seats. "Here's my number."

Chaco pulled out his Netpad and strolled past a long line of club warriors. Many were dressed like the gothic art militia, while others appeared to have just come from work. He climbed the steep granite steps and approached one of the bouncers.

"Can I help you?" the guy asked. He was bald and draped in a cloak the color of blood. Its tall white collar made his head seem like it was balanced atop a red mountain.

"What do you know?" Chaco asked flippantly. He could see his reflection in the guy's ocular implants.

The bouncer considered him with a heavy dose of apathy. "That I'm about throw an arrogant tourist onto his ass. What are you doing?" On the word "you," he leaned into Chaco's face.

"Arresting a big fucking dumbshit for obstructing a federal officer." Chaco displayed his holobadge.

The bouncer didn't react and motioned him in. Chaco walked past and barely heard him say "Asshole" over the pounding music.

The club's foyer had been converted into a staging area for the desperate. When Chaco entered, another bouncer approached. This guy was as big as the previous one and dressed exactly the same, right down to the moustache. He had his hand cupped around the side of his face, probably reading information being fed to his implants.

"Right this way," he said, not gracing Chaco with his attention.

Since his head was the only evidence of a human underneath the robe, bouncer number two seemed to float as he led Chaco along the edge of the main sanctuary. The aisle they walked was demarcated only by the fact that people never stepped into it. The club pulsated with the harsh sounds of Arabic techno, and while pockets of people were dancing, most of the crowd seemed to be standing around. Chaco and the bouncer finally reached what would've been the pulpit and mounted a set of wide stairs that looked like the same wood as the front doors. When the bouncer ascended, his floating act became even more convincing.

The stairs emptied into a large balconied room, furnished mainly with elaborate, floor-standing candelabras that held about 50 tiny white candles. Two life-size crucifixes, whose Christ figures stared mournfully up to the rafters, gated the entrance to the room. As they stepped through, the noise from the main floor dropped away. They rounded another pair of candelabras and approached a small man, dressed as a priest, sitting between two bioenhanced brunettes on a red couch the size of Lichtenstein.

"Mr. Del Mar," the bouncer announced. "Agent Sonny Chaco, National Security Agency." He then floated across the room to another set of stairs and descended to the main floor, where the frantic dance crowd swallowed him.

"Welcome to Heaven," Del Mar said with what sounded like a German accent.

"I wouldn't call it that, but thanks," Chaco replied.

"Please, sit." Del Mar motioned, and one of the brunettes scooted down the couch. Chaco took her place, careful not to get too comfortable. "You're dry." Del Mar gestured in the air, and suddenly an Asian waitress appeared and bowed.

"I'll have a beer, please," Chaco said. "And no gen enhancements."

The waitress bowed again and hurried off.

The brunette slid over and snuggled a little too closely against Chaco. Her weight pulled his coat and exposed the Light-Force holster.

Del Mar's eyes flared. "And how may I help the government?" he asked, whereupon he flourished a kiss upon the cheek of the brunette next to him. All the while, his eyes remained on Chaco.

"I've been following someone who's entered your club, and I need to stay on her. All I want to do is observe."

"And why should I help the NSA?"

Chaco took a casual account of the room. "I'm a Net Operative, Mr. Del Mar, and I'm sure there's plenty of history I could dig up on Heaven." Chaco's attention settled on a small painting nestled in a narrow alcove on a far wall. It was expensively displayed; its lone halogen caused the Madonna's face to radiate off the canvas. "You do have complete records on all of your artwork?"

Del Mar's look softened. He motioned to a dark area of the room, and a man dressed in a black leather suit emerged and approached. He had the same implants as the bouncers. Chaco figured they were all Net linked and tricked out with enhancements like VL holovision. He handed Del Mar a Netpad.

Del Mar passed it along. "Here, agent. Point her out."

Chaco took the Netpad and began scanning through images of everyone who had entered the club. They had been captured from the waist up, probably by the first bouncer's optics, and many had information boxes that detailed addresses, ages, food allergies, and drug preferences, among other things. Chaco passed Deja's image, then Corazon's (with Pavia trailing), and then his. He stopped on an image of a cute black girl, her hair teased sky high and her eyes styled like she had just stepped out of the current revival of *Cats*. He handed the Netpad back.

"Do we know her, Tommy?" Del Mar asked when he passed the Netpad to the man in black leather.

The leather guy studied the image. "I've always wondered about her," he said and pocketed the Netpad somewhere behind him. "What's she done?"

"You name it," Chaco said.

The leather guy smirked. "Figures." He turned and slipped back into the darkness.

"So, can I go about my business?" Chaco asked, taking his beer from the Asian waitress.

Del Mar spread his arms. "Welcome to my father's house."

Chaco stood and raised his bottle. "Thank you, Mr. Del Mar." The brunette next to Chaco also stood and slipped her arm through his.

"Keitha, please," Del Mar said. "Agent Chaco works alone."

She frowned childishly and sat.

Chaco passed through the crucifixes, and the music grew until he could feel it pounding inside his chest. He walked back up the aisle where the bouncer had led him, ever so often glancing into the crowd to see if he could catch a glimpse of Deja. He saw an opening between some Goth warriors and stepped through. As he pushed his way, people bumped into him, and a few felt the Light-Force because they instantly shot him a look that started at his chest before moving to his face. These people quickly shuffled away.

Chaco finally came to what he assumed was the main bar.

It was surrounded by dance-scene types. He began to circle it casually when he came upon the back of a very large guy in a black fedora.

Pavia.

Chaco quickly stepped up to a couple at the bar who looked deep in a conversation, although he had no idea how they could've managed that, what with the club's music obliterating the ability to hear. Pavia moved, which exposed Deja and Corazon, who were standing together with drinks in their hands. Deja leaned into Corazon and said something that caused Corazon to turn and speak to Pavia. They all began inching their way through the crowd away from the bar.

Chaco discreetly followed as they continued to the far side of the sanctuary. They approached another bouncer who appeared to be guarding a dozen glassed rooms that lined the edge of the dance floor. Chaco guessed that at one time these must have been side chapels, but now they were private party rooms. The whole scene was beginning to punch against his sense of morality when someone tapped his shoulder. It was the leather guy.

"We have the girl you're looking for monitored," he said.

"Good," Chaco said. "Keep an eye on her until I'm done here."

"And what, exactly, are you doing here?"

"Government business," Chaco said, this time with as much authority as he could project over the music.

The leather guy gave him a nod, then talked into the air and walked back into the crowd.

Fucking Boy Scout. Chaco went back to spying on Deja, who was now talking with the bouncer. Pavia was next to her, seemingly arguing with Corazon. They had an exchange that ended with Corazon shaking her head. Pavia stormed away and headed straight towards Chaco.

Shit. Chaco spun into a rather plain-looking girl who seemed to be having about as much fun with Heaven as a migraine. "Hi, ah, my name's Sonny. Can I buy you a drink?"

"Sure," she said, brightening. "I'm Taylor-Reese, with a dash."

"What would you like?" He watched out of the corner of his eye as Pavia stormed past.

She giggled. "A *Dee*troit Dragon."

Chaco tried to watch Deja and Corazon while ordering drinks from the bartender.

Taylor-Reese picked up on it and followed his line of sight. "Who are they?" she demanded and folded her arms.

Chaco turned back from ordering and watched Deja and Corazon disappear into one of the party rooms.

"Well?" she pressed.

Chaco forced a smile. "Okay, here's the deal.... I'm a government agent, and that's my–"

"Oh, please! You are such an asshole." She turned and

marched off.

"Mr. Asshole, no dash," Chaco said to her back. He leaned against the bar and trained his attention on the dark curtains that covered the windows of Deja and Corazon's party room.

"What happened to your friend?" the bartender asked, setting their drinks down.

Chaco shrugged and picked up his beer. The bartender laughed and dumped the Detroit Dragon into a sink.

Heaven was clearly the place to be if you were rich, chic, and could afford to get up any time past noon. Chaco sipped his beer and watched some of New York's finest clubbers do what they did best, which in Heaven meant getting as shitfaced as they could and dancing with whomever they could, for as long as they could. And if they weren't dancing, they huddled together in little cliques. When the musical selection was quieter, Chaco could overhear parts of conversations, which ranged anywhere from foreign policy to a knockdown, drag-out fight over the best handbag designer in Europe.

No one had entered or exited Deja and Corazon's party room for the last 30 minutes, and Chaco hadn't seen any evidence of Pavia in the club. He was taking another sip from his beer when Del Mar strolled up with the two Marionettes. He was shorter than Chaco had guessed and had changed into a new costume – the Pope with two hookers, except his mitre had the blinking word "OPEN" running down the front. They stopped and partially blocked Chaco's view of the party room.

"Agent Chaco, how are you enjoying Heaven?" Del Mar's demeanor clearly indicated he was Riding, but Chaco couldn't tell on what, exactly.

"You've got a great club, your Eminence," Chaco said, craning around one of the brunettes.

"Everyone should have a little taste of heaven." Del Mar smiled and took a sip from his goblet. Its encrusted jewels blinked in sync with his hat.

Suddenly, a bright light flashed inside Deja and Corazon's party room. It backlit the curtains and highlighted their elaborate Gothic patterns.

"What the hell?" Chaco said, and the light flashed again. He drew his Light-Force, and his holobadge projected.

Del Mar's eyes almost popped out of their sockets. "Oh dear God," he said and crossed himself.

The taller brunette saw the Light-Force and screamed. Chaco shoved the smaller brunette out of his way and charged towards the party room. He held his weapon like he had been taught, cupped with both hands, low and to the right. The room continued to strobe.

The bouncer guard moved to stop him but saw the Light-Force and raised his hands in a gesture that said he didn't want any part of what was going down.

Chaco ran past him at full clip, skidded up to the party

room, and slammed against one of its windows. Light flashed again, and he could feel heat against his back. He whipped the curtain aside with the tip of his Light-Force and entered in one continuous motion.

A lone candle barely illuminated the dark room, and as Chaco entered, it began to flicker. Erratic shadows danced across the walls, and he could make out only slivers of details. When his eyes adjusted, he saw Deja sitting on the edge of an overstuffed leather couch. She was staring at the candle, which was in the middle of a large wooden coffee table.

"Dej," he said, "are you all right?"

Deja sat motionless. Her expression was a mix of shock and fear. As Chaco stepped closer, he noticed that her pallor was gray.

Pavia threw the curtain aside and practically ripped it from its track. He was sweating and out of breath.

"Dej," Chaco said, ignoring Pavia, "talk to me." He was now standing next to her; she was still staring. He lowered his weapon and knelt beside her. "Dej, what happened?" He gently guided a stray lock of hair from her face. Her lower lip was quivering.

"Sonny!" Pavia's voice was edged with panic. "Where's Mrs. Goya?"

Chaco peered into the shadows. "Corazon?"

Silence.

"I have no idea." He faced Deja. "Baby, what happened

to Cor?"

She didn't respond.

"Deja," Chaco said, this time more firmly, "where's Cora–"

"Marl," Deja uttered, and then threw up.

Coming into focus

21

DEJA slowly came to, although she had never really gone unconscious, just ... out of focus. Chaco wiped at the corners of her mouth with a warm towel, and there was a faint smell of vomit, like what lingered near garbage cans after a wild club party. She was sitting in an uncomfortable wooden chair in the middle of a huge restroom. Lamps that looked like torches adorned walls fashioned after a medieval castle. The flames looked real, and the walls appeared slick with moisture, but the room felt cool and dry. Pavia stood behind Chaco, along with three Hispanic chicks dressed like they were going to the prom, though they were well past that stage. Also hanging around was a creepy guy wearing the same sunglasses as the bouncers. He was dressed in black leather standing next to a nun ... at least what looked like a nun, if you discounted the piercings. Everybody wore serious expressions, especially Chaco.

"Deja, can you hear me?"

She heard, sort of. "Yeah," she tried, but her throat was raw and burning. She coughed.

"Hey," Chaco said, turning to Pavia, "she's coming around." He knelt. "Dej, can you talk?"

Deja looked into his face and managed a frail smile. She put her arms around his neck and hugged him. He held her tight and gently kissed the side of her face. Then she started crying. It was more like sobbing, although she had no idea why. She just knew she had to. Inside her, something was releasing – a catalyst that sure felt like guilt.

"It's okay, baby. Let it out," Chaco said softly.

Deja's mind was spinning as she remembered the party room, the bright flashing light, and the reason for her need to cry.

Pavia's knees cracked as he knelt. He placed his hand on her shoulder; his touch was remarkably gentle. "How do you feel?" he asked.

"Like crap," she replied.

Chaco tossed the towel at the base of a trashcan. The girl dressed as a nun walked over with another. He thanked her and began dabbing at Deja's tears. "Do you want some water?" he asked.

She nodded.

The nun poured a glass of water from a ceramic pitcher and handed it to Deja before bowing slightly and returning to her place.

Deja sipped from the glass, and the cool water washed away the burning in her throat. "Did I puke or something?"

Chaco smiled. "Yeah," he said. "Kind of all over yourself."

Deja examined the front of her dress and winced.

"Deja," Pavia said, giving her shoulder a squeeze, "where's Mrs. Goya?"

She hesitated, suddenly feeling the stares, and cautiously scanned the room.

"All right," Chaco said, "everyone out of here!"

As the last Hispanic prom girl left the restroom, Chaco stepped over to the guy in leather. "You too," he ordered. "And I don't want anyone coming in here." The guy actually saluted, and Chaco began to return it before he waved him off. He walked back to Deja, knelt, and gently took her hands.

"Okay, that's everyone," he said. "Now, Dej, I need you to tighten up here. What happened?"

"I-I don't know where to begin."

"Deja," Pavia said earnestly, "the next few hours are critical. We need to know what's going on."

Deja took another drink of water, then told Chaco and Pavia everything, starting from when she first met Corazon on the jump jet, to the bar with Torres, and finally to her bizarre encounter with Marl on the streets of New York, which she still wasn't convinced took place anywhere but her mind.

"Okay, then," Chaco said. "Now, what happened in the party room?"

"I was telling Cor the same stuff I just told you," Deja said. "I was right at the part about Marl wanting to meet with her and all when the room filled with this unbelievable white light. It was flashing and popping, and then ..." Deja's throat tightened, and her head began to throb.

"Dej, honey," Chaco urged, "come on. I need you to remember."

"And then ... she was gone, Sonny. Just *gone*."

Chaco and Pavia exchanged glances.

"Deja," Pavia said, "are you on any drugs?"

"No, she's not!" Chaco said with such authority that even Pavia was taken aback.

Chaco stood and started pacing. "This is way out of my league," he muttered. He stopped and folded his arms. "Let me get this straight. We're dealing with a lovesick clone-thing who communicates inside people's heads, and who just kidnapped the wife-clone of one of the most prominent businessmen in the country?" He emphasized this last thought with a pointed finger.

"I'm going to be fired." He threw his hands up. "Hell, I'm going to disappear!" He started pacing again.

"Now it's your turn to tighten up," Pavia said.

"Easy for you to say. You're not in the system anymore."

Pavia rested a hand on Chaco's shoulder. "Like it or not, this is your case, and we're losing time."

"I know, I know." Chaco took a deep breath. "You told me you might have a way to get to this clone."

"No," Pavia said. "I was just posturing. I don't have dick on this guy."

"Sonny," Deja said, her voice back from the dead, "is there anybody in your unit who could help?"

"Exposing all this could be catastrophic," Chaco said. "If what you say this clone can do is real, then we could be dealing with a whole new type of weapon. No," he said, shaking his head, "I may need to go to DoD with this."

"Then you *will* disappear," Pavia replied.

Chaco put his face into his hands and began rubbing his forehead. The room fell deathly quiet, and Deja's heart went out to her lover. He had been so strong, barking orders and taking charge. But now, he looked utterly lost.

"Wait a minute," Chaco said through his fingers. "Dej, you might be right." He grabbed his coat off a chair in the corner. "Pavia," he said, slipping it on, "I need to get into some VirtGear, and it needs to be military issue, not any cheap civilian crap."

Pavia smiled broadly for the first time. "Now that I can help you with."

Chaco kissed Deja on the forehead and helped her up. "Thank you," he whispered, and as they hurried from the restroom, he said something under his breath, something that just didn't make any sense.

"Ghost in the machine?"

You'll have my best

22

TSUKAHARA passionately pressed his lips against Miko's. They had danced around their feelings for so long that being this close was exciting, yet intensely awkward. He had never felt this way for another girl, and the fact that she didn't care about his weight only added to the genuineness of the moment.

"Oh, Yoichi," she said, pulling back to take him in. Her eyes were dark and set a bit close, and Tsukahara loved the way they were slightly crossed, especially when they kissed. It gave her an innocence that he could fall in love with so easily. He kissed her again.

Miko gently pulled him towards her bed. "I have something for you," she said with a slight giggle. She slipped out of her sandals and neatly arranged them with her foot at the base of the bed. She pulled back the covers, sat, and began unbuttoning her blouse, which clung perfectly to her delicate breasts.

He tried to help her.

"Hey, Tsuka!"

Tsukahara surfaced from his dream to find the soft glow of an incoming holo call hovering at the foot of his bed. The side of his face was buried in his pillow; his cheek pressed against a wet drool spot. He quickly sat up and wiped the side of his mouth.

"I didn't wake you, did I?" Chaco asked.

"No, sir," Tsukahara said. He realized the mound in his sweat pants and quickly gathered the sheets around his waist. "I had just gone to bed. What time is it?"

"Time to get to the virtlab, agent. I've got business that needs your attention ... and only yours."

As Tsukahara's eyes adjusted, he noticed the holojection transmission was the type that field operatives used only when they felt their lives might be in danger. It was highly secure and transmitted not only the imaging signal, but the operative's medical information and sometimes physical location, as well. A shot of adrenaline coursed through his nerves.

"Where are you, sir?" Tsukahara asked. Chaco was in the back of what appeared to be a large car with a girl next to him. She was very pretty and dressed in a businesslike manner with a touch of street chic. She also had crazy hair that shifted colors as the car passed under streetlights.

"I'm still in New York, and, oh, sorry ... this is Deja Moriarty. Deja, Yoichi Tsukahara. He's the one I was telling you about."

Tsukahara gave a quick, sharp bow of his head.

The pretty girl waved tentatively, and her hair shifted color again.

"What security level are you with incomings?" Chaco asked.

"The highest."

"Good, 'cause this assignment is very 'out of system,' if you get my drift. I want you to get down to the lab and into some secure V-Gear, and don't use Davis's, use mine. You'll find it in my office. It's the latest, and we're going to need all the muscle we can. You with me?" Chaco and the pretty girl suddenly bounced together, which was odd because most major road surfaces had been redone with FLEX technology in their polymers.

Tsukahara sat up straighter and brushed hair off his face. "Yes, sir."

"I'm sending you the coordinates for our meeting room, along with my office's security code. If anyone gives you shit about being in my office, tell 'em you're doing a Code 12 for me.

They won't bother you after that." Chaco entered the data into his Netpad, and it simultaneously appeared to the left of his image. "Be there in an exactly one hour."

Tsukahara climbed out of bed and stumbled toward his closet.

"Oh, and ah, Tsuka?"

He snapped to attention. "Yes, sir?"

"This one's important. No bullshit here. I need you at your very best." His superior's heart rate, which was tracking in the upper right of the transmission along with 11 other med readings, jumped.

"Don't worry, sir," Tsukahara answered with a slight bow. "You'll have my best."

The pretty girl snuggled against Chaco's shoulder, and he kissed the top of her head. His heart rate lowered.

"See you in an hour," Chaco said, and his heart rate spiked again.

That's comforting  23

"**WHERE** the hell are we?" Chaco asked.

"The Garden State," Pavia said.

"Pennsylvania?"

"No, Sonny, we're in Jersey," Deja said sleepily from the back of the car. She uncurled herself from her nap and glanced at her watch. "And judging by the time," she said through a yawn, "I'd say we're south, around ... Atlantic City?"

"Very good, Ms. Moriarty," Pavia said.

"What's in Atlantic City?" Chaco asked.

Pavia tapped in a number, and the car's main monitor activated. The NetCom logo faded in, followed by an image of a tensile little man who looked nervous and strung out. He coughed, and oily black hair fell across his gaunt face.

"You up?" Pavia asked.

"Hell, yes," the man replied through another cough.

"We're 15 minutes away, so you better be–"

"I'll be ready, Oscar. Don't worry." The man hacked, and his image cut out.

"*He's* going help us?" Chaco asked.

"That guy can out-Net you any day of the week."

"What's his name?" Deja asked, inspecting the damage from her nap with a compact mirror.

"Bartas," Pavia replied.

"Bartas who?"

"Pavia."

Deja lowered the mirror. "He's your brother?"

Pavia's jaw grinded. "Yes."

"You say that like you're ashamed."

Chaco read aloud from his Netpad: "Pavia, Bartas C. Age: 43. Born: Mexico City, Mexico. Current Residence: Atlantic City, New Jersey. Ah, here we go. Military Service: Army. Special Ops. Net Operative. Code Reader. Nodal Point Specialist. Data Profiler." He scanned further. "We have a lot in common."

"Great," Pavia said. "You can bond."

"Wife: Sezja M. Born: St. Petersburg, Russia. Age: 38. Child: *Oscar*. Born: Washington D.C. Age: 9 –" Chaco read the next entry to himself.

"What is it, Sonny?" Deja asked.

Chaco looked at Pavia. "Both deceased."

Pavia kept looking out the windshield.

"Their case, as of this record, is still unsolved." Chaco slowly pocketed his Netpad.

*   *   *

Somewhere near the fringe of Atlantic City, Chaco picked up the glow of casino lights reflecting against the underside of low, early morning clouds. It created the illusion that most of the Boardwalk sector was covered by a lambent dome. Pavia exited the Interway and entered a residential area that looked like it might have been a pleasant place to live 20 years ago. He piloted the car for about a mile before he turned into an old storage park, the kind popular when the middle class needed a place to store the excesses of indulgent consumerism. The car skirted endless rows of units that had been converted into residences, although, judging by the trash and general disrepair, Chaco deduced they weren't for the upwardly mobile.

Pavia edged down one of the narrow streets and glided past

roll door after roll door, all painted the same pathetic gray. Each unit had a fixture that illuminated a makeshift front porch – or what passed for one, considering it was just large enough for a chair and, in some cases, an old temperature-based refrigerator.

They stopped close to the middle of the row and parked in front of a unit whose crudely stenciled numbers labeled it "289."

"So, this is beautiful Atlantic City?" Chaco asked, stretching.

"More like its underbelly," Pavia replied. He moved around the back of the car and approached the front door.

Oddly, it was colonial style, complete with an ornate brass doorknob and knocker. An old WELCOME mat made out of the same bright green plastic shit that Chaco's dad had glued to the front steps of their old house greeted them. Part of a big daisy clung to its upper left corner, and all that was left of "welcome" was WE--OM-. The door had been poorly retrofitted into the metal roll door and was the only one of its kind, as far as Chaco could see.

"I'd heard that people were living in these old parks, but I didn't think it was true," he said.

"People are living in these all over the country," Pavia said while he pressed the doorbell. Three deadbolts unlocked in sequence, and the porch light flickered.

The walls and carpet hid any indication that three, possibly four, units had been merged into one. The foyer they entered was poorly lit and crammed with old electronic equipment, stacks of brown boxes, and antique paper magazines. Chaco caught a glimpse of a vintage issue of *Wired* in the dim light. The whole place smelled musty, like his uncle's basement where he and his cousins had played elaborate spy games as kids. The space had been cheaply finished and reminded Chaco of a prefab apartment he visited at an aqua-park in Jersey, except those had been the size of a closet and were stacked and glued together by the hundreds.

"Hello, brother," a voice said from the dreariness.

"Bartas," Pavia deadpanned.

Bartas Pavia's stooped figure came up the long hallway that emptied into the foyer. The hallway had two doors on each side and split the space down the middle. The kitchen was at the other end, and the glow from the counter lights cast Bartas into silhouette. He was wearing an old bathrobe, the flannel kind you might wear in the dead of winter. Chaco also recognized a smell, isolating it from the dank residue that was collecting in his sinuses. Sickness.

The two men embraced, but not like brothers. Their hug had more resemblance to two businessmen about to enter negotiations.

Deja stepped closer to Chaco. He took her hand.

"Oscar, you must be in a hell of a jam to ask for my help." Bartas tightened the robe around what little body was left on his frame.

"I am, brother, and you know I wouldn't come if it wasn't important."

Bartas laughed, which triggered a coughing fit. Deja stepped forward, but Chaco squeezed her hand to signal her to hold her ground. Pavia, void of any compassion, just observed.

Bartas motioned for them to follow. He led them down the hallway and into a room filled with an eclectic array of NetLink router hubs, virtual hard drives, a small omni-processing main frame, and a Net console the likes of which Chaco had never seen. The room hummed with an electronic pulse.

"Please, sit," Bartas said with a raspiness that made Chaco want to slap on a micropore mask.

Bartas collapsed into an old chair and casually eyed his guests. "Didn't you tell them, Oscar?"

"It wouldn't have mattered," Pavia replied.

"Excuse me." Deja said. She looked questioningly at Bartas. "How long have you had ... Netox?"

"Deja!" Chaco said. "That doesn't exist. It's just media hype."

"The hell it is" Bartas replied. "Look at your future, agent." He gestured at his own body.

"There's no scientific proof that Netox exists. I've read the studies ... even the classified ones." Chaco glowered at Deja. "And how do you know so much about it?"

"I care for you, Sonny," Deja said. "I just wanted to learn

about anything that might harm you."

"You should listen to her," Bartas said. "She's a smart girl."

Chaco turned to Deja. "I'm very protected when I'm in the Net. The data buffers and virus filters we use are state-of-the-art."

"Bullshit!" Bartas said. "That's what I thought, but ten years later, look how the buffers and filters protected me." He coughed and pulled his robe tightly around his neck. "What they aren't telling you is that data pathogens will get through.... They're way below the threshold. They'll slowly attack your nervous system." He eyed Chaco. "Then one morning you'll wake up and have this feeling. At first, you'll think you've got the flu, but then you realize that the shaking and the fever and the dreams are the result of your nervous system breaking down." He leaned forward, and his hands reacted to a tremor that rippled through him. "But by then," he said gravely, "you're screwed."

"Yes, well, that's only partly explains your condition," Pavia said. "And we're not here to convince Agent Chaco that Netox exits. He'll have to figure that out on his own." He stepped over to the console and ran his fingers across its interface panel. "We're here, Bartas, because we have to find–"

"Your employer's missing wife. Yes, you told me all about it," Bartas said. "What's the matter, brother, losing your touch?"

"What we're losing is time," Chaco said. "Bartas, I need to use your VirtGear to connect with one of my agents. I might be in for a long time."

Bartas gestured at the console. "Knock yourself out. But I'll warn you, this is a custom unit. It's not going to act like that crap you're used to at the NSA."

Chaco joined Pavia and reviewed the system's interface controls. "I may need your help with this equipment," Chaco said.

"Don't worry, agent. I'll be in there with you. Now just sit in that chair." Bartas pointed to what looked like an ordinary recliner positioned in the only open space available in the cramped room.

"Isn't it dangerous for you to go back into the Net?" Deja asked.

Bartas shot her a look. "In my condition, do you really think it matters? Besides, it's the only place I can still get a little entertainment." He winked.

Chaco climbed into the chair and waited while it adjusted to his body's contour. "Where's the unit?" he said, inspecting the armrests.

Bartas smiled for the first time. "It's the chair."

Chaco searched the chair, even looking to see if he was sitting on it.

"It *is* the chair," Bartas reiterated.

"Really?"

"A little different, isn't it?" Bartas pointed. "Set your coordinates, then on my mark touch the red button on the interface panel, but only when you're ready. It packs more of a punch than you're used to."

Pavia sat next to Deja on a small couch and patted her knee.

Bartas raised a standard VirtGear unit to his forehead. "This should be interesting," he muttered through a cough.

Chaco examined the chair's system panel and entered the coordinates for the meeting room. He took a deep breath and leaned back. "I'm ready."

"On my mark," Bartas said. "Three, two ... *one*."

Chaco clicked the red button, and the chair awoke into a kind of full-body VirtGear. Tentacles at least three times as thick as a standard head model emerged from under the armrests. They crawled across Chaco's body, and it took every bit of his willpower not to leap from the chair. When a tentacle found its contact point, its head articulated like the mouth of a tiny snake, bit through Chaco's clothes, and pricked the surface of his skin with a needlelike inceptor. One tentacle hovered in front of his face, but then separated into six smaller ones that wrapped themselves around his head. The whole action happened so fast that the interface process was complete before Chaco could scream.

"Hello, agent."

Chaco's vision faded in, and he found himself standing in the NSA's virtual meeting room. It had been simmed to represent a typical conference room found on any floor of the Maryland headquarters. Bartas was standing across the table, but here he was clean-shaven and about 60 pounds heavier. He sported an expensive biosuit, and his hair was cut in a contemporary style. Chaco figured it must be how he looked before his illness.

"Hello, Bartas. You're looking—"

"Like I used to. Surprising, isn't it?"

Chaco shrugged.

"Where's your agent?"

Tsukahara materialized to the left of Chaco, facing away from the table. He quickly turned and bowed. "With apologies."

"Don't sweat it, Tsuka. I've done that a million times." Chaco noticed his intern had puzzled look. "Is there something wrong?"

"Sir, your form. It's so ... real."

Bartas snickered.

Chaco looked down at his body for the first time and felt his arms. "Jesus, I can feel!" He touched the tabletop, picked up a Netpad, and ran his fingers over its control panel. "This is amazing!"

"Total Body Interface Function," Bartas said. He walked around the table and offered his hand. "Welcome to the future of the Net."

Chaco eyed his hand before he shook it. "Whoa, I can even feel your pulse. Is this your invention?"

Bartas smiled. "With a little help from some friends in the Baltics."

Tsukahara touched Chaco's shoulder. "It still feels the same for me.... That is, I have no feeling."

"Right," Bartas said, "only Agent Chaco has full sensory capacity. Someday, everyone will."

Chaco looked at his watch. "Tsuka, the last time you were in the Net, you said you came in contact with a presence, right?"

Tsukahara cautiously nodded.

"Do you think you could contact it again?"

"I can try, sir."

"What," Bartas said, "you think this presence is the clone you're looking for?"

"Possibly," Chaco said.

"That's a long shot."

"No. I've got a feeling here. Did your brother tell you everything?"

"Superclone stumps one of NSA's finest? Yeah, he told me. But do you really think it's a weapon?"

"This thing has a pretty impressive bag of tricks – like appearing and disappearing at will. And I'm not talking about in the Net."

Bartas's brow furrowed.

"I'm just telling you what I saw," Chaco said. "When we jack out, ask Deja. She was there."

"Come on," Bartas said. "This thing can't just vaporize and reappear. If you're talking about something like quantum teleportation, they canned that concept years ago. Don't get me wrong. It was cool when that group at MIT transported the dog, but all they got was a copy. Hell, they had to reteach it everything, even how to take a crap."

"Look, all I'm saying is this clone is capable of things I've never seen before."

"Okay," Bartas said. "Say, for the sake of argument, it is what you say. What are you going to do, ask it to cooperate?"

"Yeah ... basically."

"One of NSA's finest," Bartas said. He made himself comfortable in a conference room chair and propped his feet on top of the table.

"Tsuka, Bartas and I are going to be 'one way' in this. We'll be involved, but the presence won't know we're here. You got that?"

"Yes, sir."

"All right, then. Go and do whatever you did last time, and if you get into any trouble, we'll jump in."

Tsukahara bowed.

Bartas rolled his eyes. "That's comforting."

This is not how I imagined it

24

TSUKAHARA watched Bartas and his superior, along with the NSA meeting room, dissolve to leave him floating quietly amidst streams of data. He closed his eyes and opened his mind to the chi of the presence he had previously encountered. The fate of his career might hang on the success of this assignment, and the thought of returning to Japan in disgrace only fueled his drive to make contact.

Tsukahara had convinced himself that the presence was

PAUL BLACK

an AI interface whose programming had evolved beyond the legal
limitations of The Hague Artificial Intelligence Accords. Now,
however, his superior informed him that the presence might be a
new form of cloned human – very powerful and possibly a threat
to national security – and that he might be its first official contact.
Tsukahara was honored to be granted such an important
assignment, and as he floated among the streams of data, he
wondered if the presence was truly a new form of cloned human.
And if it was a threat, which country had created it? If only his
colleagues back at the Japanese National Security Agency could
see him now. If only his mother could.

She would be proud, Yoichi.

The Net jittered, and suddenly Tsukahara found himself
standing by the stream near his family's old cottage in Hakuba. It
was spring, and the smell of adonis, zazensou, and dogtooth violets
filled the air. A cool breeze played through the trees. Then a shiver
ran through his body, though he didn't know if the wind or the
presence had caused it.

"Are you the entity I encountered before?" Tsukahara
asked.

Yes, I am, the voice replied in perfect Japanese. It echoed
in his mind as if part of him.

"Then I need–"

Do you like your environment?

The summers Tsukahara had spent in Hakuba were the

happiest times of his life, and the setting was just the way he remembered it, even down to the small wooden bridge that spanned the stream. In reality, his father had died before he could build the bridge, but in Tsukahara's memory, it was always there.

"Yes, I do. I see that you have extrapolated this simulation from my memory. How did–?"

I thought you would be more comfortable.

"Thank you. Yes, I am." Tsukahara bowed, wondering how the presence had scanned his memory. He sensed that certain questions might remain unanswered. "I've been asked to–"

Corazon Goya is well and in no danger.

A spark of fear cut through Tsukahara with the realization that his superior's hunch had been correct. He focused on the presence. "When will you release Ms. Goya?"

A bird passed overhead. Tsukahara watched its small black form maneuver through the trees. It tucked its wings and glided onto a thin branch, which bobbed gently from its weight. The scene was so convincing that, for a brief moment, Tsukahara longed for the summers at his family's cottage.

Why don't you ask me what's really on your mind?

Tsukahara hesitated. "My superior wishes to know who or what you are. Are you a threat to the security of New America?"

There was a pause. Tsukahara walked closer to the stream.

Not in the sense that you define a threat. It is not primary to my mission.

A mission? "What is your mission?"

To affect change.

"How?"

By setting into motion a cascade effect that will bring about balance.

Tsukahara was confused. If the clone wasn't a threat – although it appeared to have a mission – then what was it? What kind of cascade effect was it referring to, and what would be brought into balance? He began to suspect that he was dialoguing with a new form of artificial intelligence, possibly one that had lost control of its rational programming. But even if the interface had become corrupt, it should be able to reprogram itself … unless it didn't know it had become corrupt. Yet that, too, seemed highly unlikely. A shocking consideration then came into Tsukahara's mind, and his heart began to race.

I sense you are scared, Yoichi.

"You're not from our planet … are you?"

Another pause. The bird launched off the branch and ascended in a graceful arc to the tops of the trees.

Not in the sense that you would understand. The ones who created me occupy the space between planets.

Tsukahara's heart was pounding against his chest, and his hands were shaking. He was desperately trying to wrap his prudent mind around the enormity of the revelation.

This was first contact.

He began to take deep gulping breaths in a desperate attempt to calm his nerves.

What troubles you, Yoichi?

Tsukahara had never dreamed that first contact would be in the virtual realm of the Net. As a boy, he imagined it would be like the movies, albeit the depictions he had grown up with were foolish, and the idea of spaceships and spindly gray men seemed rather arrogant now. Obviously, a race of higher intelligence would choose a more controllable venue to reveal its existence, and what better environment than the Net?

Tsukahara swallowed and found his throat dry. "Y-Yes ... I mean no–"

Yoichi?

"Yes?"

Don't be afraid.

"Why are you–"

The ones who created me are the ones who set into motion the first cascade, which gave way to the rise of man. They now wish to correct the imbalances that have occurred and have sent me to affect change.

"How will you do this?"

There was another long pause, and Tsukahara felt he might not get an answer. Having calmed himself, he recalled the line of questioning Chaco had instructed him to pursue. "Why did you take Ms. Goya?"

She chose to be with me.

"Why, then, is it important that she be with you?"

To help.

"How can she?"

Another pause, and another bird.

I believe she is the connection for me to understand how your world's belief systems work, and thus, how to set into motion the effect. You know that what I need to do is important, Yoichi.

Tsukahara was at a loss for words. He did want change. For the last 50 years, the world had been slowly cracking apart at its cultural seams. The Biolution and its heralded flood of technology was supposed to have been the great equalizing force that was to close the gap between the haves and the have-nots. But since its development, it actually had created an even greater divide, one that now pitted the secure against the desperate. Tsukahara's mind was spinning.

I sense you are worried, Yoichi. Don't be. Your world will never know of the implementation. The effect will, in time, lead your world off its current path of self-destruction.

"Why now? Why not another time, like the opening of the atomic age?"

The advancement you call the Biolution is a more accessible threat. Your world is no longer a collection of independent cultures. It has become a vastly interconnected organism, yet it still operates within archaic religious and political models. With this advancement, your world's scientific communities are about to discover the next set of universal governing laws.

"Like a new branch of quantum theory?"

No, Yoichi. What you call theoretical physics only explains a fraction of the universe.

Tsukahara sensed the presence was slipping away. He only had a rudimental knowledge of quantum physics, and to continue down this path was a waste of precious time. "My superior wants to know when Ms. Goya will be returned."

She can return whenever she wishes.

At a loss, Tsukahara was distracted by the stream at his feet. He knelt and cut the surface with his hand. Crescents of sunlight rippled out; he could feel the water's chill as it flowed through his fingers; a small koi swam just beyond his reach. He was overwhelmed.

What troubles you, Yoichi? The voice was now softer.

"This isn't how I imagined it would be," Tsukahara said under his breath. He watched the koi swim a semicircle and dart from view; another bird flew overhead; its image tracked erratically across the surface of the disrupted water.

Yoichi. The presence was now just barely audible inside his head. *Many things in life ever are.*

You've lost your color

25

DEJA opened her eyes.

She was in Chaco's bed at The Thin. Small red numerals outlined in magenta floated above the side table. *6:56 p.m.*

She remembered.

After watching Chaco and Bartas twitch in their seats for an hour, she and Pavia had gone into his brother's kitchen to find something to drink. When they returned, Chaco and Bartas were disengaged from the Net and huddled talking. She had been relieved to hear that Cor was safe and apparently acting of her own free will, but Chaco was pissed that he and Bartas hadn't been able to eavesdrop on Tsukahara's meeting. It had something to do with being "walled-up," whatever that meant. They also weren't buying into Tsukahara's story, which was pretty bizarre. Pavia had become very agitated, going on about his duty and how "they" wouldn't understand all this. To Deja, it didn't make any sense that Marl was some kind of alien. Then again, he seemed to have powers that were beyond those of a military clone. Usually, they were just hyper-humans developed for specific tasks, such as covert operations or risky space trips. Clones like Cor, on the other hand, were developed to fulfill some rich person's emotional needs, a practice outlawed years ago.

Being in the Net had clearly taken its toll on Pavia's brother, who had excused himself to go lay down. He had sweated profusely through the length of the session, and the smell of his sickness had grown more acrid. It was the same odor that had filled her aunt's bedroom the week before she died of TR Syndrome.

Chaco and Pavia would have stayed all day, working out their plans and making Net calls, if Deja hadn't laid down the law. Besides, what did they hope to accomplish against an alien who could manipulate matter and read minds?

The numbers on the bedside clock dissolved to 7:00 p.m.

"Hey, sleepy head," Chaco said. "Time to rise and shine." He pulled the curtains aside to let the sunset flood the room. A thick layer of ash from the offshore garbage kilns had turned the sky a deep red, and dark blue storm clouds lent the whole scene a morbid translucency.

"Sonny, close those," Deja said before she covered her eyes. "I'm going to melt." She was in one of Chaco's shirts, and his musk permeated the fabric.

He sat next to her and eclipsed the light. "How do you feel?"

"Better. I really needed a nap."

"Me, too. It's been a long day." He took her hand.

"Sonny ... what are you going to do?"

Chaco sighed and shook his head. "The problem is, I don't really know what I'm dealing with. The chances of Marl actually being an alien are remote. I think Tsuka is reading way too much into this. And even if Marl is, my hands are tied. I can't go to my boss. He's so conservative he makes Alberts look liberal. And I certainly can't go to DoD. Pavia's right. I would disappear." He sighed again, and Deja started rubbing his fingers. "He's got to be homegrown," Chaco said in a tone that betrayed the fact he was trying to convince himself. "The only thing I can figure is that he's some kind of distraction. I think he's a plant from the Pac-Rim Triad. It would be their style to imbed a clone like him. They'd love to get us going off on some tangent while they're jerkin' with our interests on the other side of the world."

"But, Sonny," Deja said, snuggling closer, "what if Marl

is an alien?"

Chaco searched her face with a sense of loss behind his eyes. "If that's the case," he said just above a whisper, "then nothing will ever be the same again."

*   *   *

The hydroshower's wall of water gushed over Deja's body. The mix of forced air, water, and three different lotions slammed against her with just enough pressure to massage away the stiffness from spending over an hour curled up in the back of Pavia's car.

"Sonny?" she called when she emerged. She lost herself in an oversized towel. *"Sonny?"*

Deja walked to the coffee table and picked through the remains of dinner. There was a handwritten note stuck into a small mound of untouched guacamole.

Went for a walk to get my head clear on all this. Hang out and relax, the room is yours. I'll be back soon.
~ Sonny

Deja tried one of Chaco's French fries but couldn't really distinguish any significant difference from her own version, even though his had been prepared to his genetic tastes. That simple fact confirmed her suspicions that all the biofood crap was just a big scam. She mopped up the last of the catsup with a limp fry and settled into one of the room's oversized loungers.

"Request. Guide," she said to the room's com system.

The large impressionistic painting of a Paris street scene morphed into The Thin's logo, whereupon the screen split into a patchwork of individual channel frames and service icons offered by the hotel. She scanned the frames until she found *Life's a Bitch*. The screen filled with episode 46, a rerun from two seasons ago. She watched for barely a minute before the room announced that someone was at the door.

"Who is it?" she asked.

"There is no identification, Ms. Moriarty."

"Give me a visual." The screen morphed again, and Corazon's distorted face pixeled up.

Deja bounded across the room and almost stumbled out of the towel. The door slid aside. "Cor!" she exclaimed, and embraced her.

"Oh, Deja," Corazon said, returning the hug, "I have so much to tell you!"

"Are you all right? You're not hurt, are you?"

"No, dear, I'm fine."

They sat on the couch, and Deja couldn't help but stare at Corazon's orange rings. Her mind went back to the night at the club and the party booth.

"Deja, what is it?"

"I'm sorry, Cor," Deja answered. "I feel so responsible for getting you into this mess. You could have been killed."

"My dear, first off, I was never in any danger. I went because I wanted to. And second, there is no *mess*. Marl is here to help. He only wants to do what's right."

"Tell that to Sonny and Mr. Pavia. They've got it in their heads that he's some kind of, I don't know, Chinese diversion in a global terrorist plan."

Corazon frowned. "They're not planning to do any thing rash, are they?"

"All I know is that they had Sonny's intern meet with Marl inside the Net, and that Marl claimed he was on a mission."

"And they didn't believe him?"

"Cor, Sonny and Mr. Pavia are cut from the same mold. They're hard-liners. They think more in terms of the real world, not something out of science fiction."

"But they have to understand. Marl is here to help."

"Cor, to tell you the truth, I find it kind of hard to believe, too. If Marl is from another world, isn't it a little weird that he sneaks around in the Net? Why didn't he just land during the World Bowl and say hello?"

"Because, Deja, I think that's the point."

"What do you mean?"

Corazon hesitated. "I don't think he did land here."

"What? No. He had to. How else would've he gotten here?

He is here ... isn't he? I mean, he was with us ... at the bar, right?"

"Was he, Deja? Was he really, *physically* with us?"

"Well, maybe ... I mean ..." Deja began to think. As wild as it sounded, every encounter with Marl could have been all in her mind. The idea made a little sense, but something didn't ring true. "I can kind of buy into the concept of him entering our thoughts," she said, "but I'll bet you that he's physically here in the city."

"Deja, the way he explained it is that his physical self is in some sort of transition. A state of projection is what he called it."

The thought of it made Deja's skin tingle. "Tell me, Cor, what's he like?"

Corazon beamed. "Deja, he's so wonderful. We have this connection, and I've never felt anything like it."

"Where did you go? I mean, one minute you were standing in front of me, and the next, you were gone. What did that feel like?"

"When he appeared, it was like we were talking, but it was inside my head. I ... I just knew I wanted to be with him. The actual act of him taking me was like going through a door." Corazon appeared unsure of her description. "Yes," she eventually said, staring and nodding, "it was just like walking through a door of light. He held my hand all the way..."

"Cor?"

"I'm sorry, dear. Where was I?"

"You walked through the door with Marl."

"Yes. Then we were on a street in the Upper West Side. Just like that. He took me to a small Italian restaurant, where we talked."

"About what?"

"Deja, it like he's searching. He asked me all about the world, about its cultures, its politics...." The spacey look returned to her face.

"Cor?"

"Why me?" Corazon said under her breath. "I'm only three years old."

Deja put her arm around her. "Probably 'cause you're the best of both worlds."

"What do you mean?"

"Think about it. You're an adult, with an adult's opinion and point of view. But you're also kind of a child. I mean, at three years old, no matter how much was programmed into you, you don't have all the baggage that comes with a lifetime of living. You have an innocence that's very rare. And I'd imagine your take on the world is a lot less judgmental than most. I envy you, Cor. You're like a new drive, free of all the crap that builds up after years of use."

Corazon shied at the analogy.

"Besides," Deja continued, "I still think he has the hots for you."

Corazon started to laugh, which got Deja going, too. For a moment, the weight of the situation was gone.

Corazon's laughter soon waned, however. "Deja," she said with a sudden urgency, "you don't think Sonny and Oscar are really going to do something to Marl, do you?"

"I don't know. I guess that all depends on whether you think Marl's here or not. If he is here, I mean physically here, then I guess they could–" But Deja cut herself off, remembering a Net call between Chaco and Pavia that she overheard. They had talked a lot of techno-speak about stuff like reverse addressing and backdoor accessing. She knew all about that stuff from her years as a news researcher. She unconsciously glanced at the note peeking from under the guacamole. "Cor," she said, the word sticking in her throat, "do you know where Marl lives? I mean, did he take you anywhere else ... after your dinner?"

"Yes. He took me to his hotel. Why?"

Deja felt a sudden arc of panic and pulled the towel tightly across her chest.

"Why Deja," Corazon said, "you've lost all your color."

It's all right  26

A strong rain pelted the windshield of the car, which wasn't
a problem for the wipers unless the storm intensified beyond a
Category 1, which was when the vehicle's intelligence core would
engage the air jets. Chaco figured the ride was probably Pavia's
personal vehicle, because it looked liked it had been through the
wringer. The car he drove to Atlantic City was out of the AztecaNet
motor pool, which was maintained by a bunch of fanatical Israelis.
Pavia had said that if he brought it back with so much as a spec of

bird shit on it, they'd go off on him and bitch that they'd have to reseal it. Ever since the attack on Central Park, who knew what was coming out of pigeons these days? Pavia was off duty, though, so tonight they were slumming it.

The ride uptown was pretty bleak, especially with Pavia doing his silent routine. Chaco hadn't much to say either, considering he wasn't too crazy about their plan. It just reeked of half-assedness, and while he didn't mind breaking from the book, he still wasn't convinced that Pavia was being completely upfront about his intentions.

Pavia's brother had come through with an address for Marl, though how was still a mystery. And even though the incept was a perfect match, the fact that the connection point was up for grabs made the idea of busting into a hotel room in the middle of the night feel very amateurish. Even so, time was against them. The system back at NSA didn't have any clearer incepts, so Chaco figured he'd go along with Pavia and hope for the best.

"That's all we need," Pavia remarked.

"What's that?" Chaco asked.

"Rain," he said, like it was root of all evil. "Just adds another element to deal with."

At this time of night, traffic was light, especially considering the weather, so movement through the city was free of the gridlock that had become a trademark for most New American cities. Even with the vast network of intelligent Interway, most inner-city streets were still uncontrolled and volatile, and it could take hours just to crawl a couple of miles.

The incept points put the connection emanating from a Harlem business hotel. An odd location, it confirmed to Chaco that their boy was homegrown. If they were really dealing with a representative from a master race, wouldn't it have picked something a little more upscale? Then again, nothing about this case surprised him anymore. At least the hotel had an all-night buffet.

"Are you sure these are correct?" Chaco asked, pointing at the SATNAV downlink on the dash.

"Bartas is rarely wrong."

Another roar of water hit the car's undercarriage, and the suspension groaned trying to prevent the vehicle from hydroplaning.

"So what happened to your brother, anyway?" Chaco asked.

Pavia glanced over and reprised the look he had on the LEV. His chin was striped with fingers of bright yellow coordinate numbers from the SATNAV panel. "He couldn't resist the easy money."

"Doing what?"

"Some shit that cost him."

"Cost him what?"

Pavia's look bordered on tragic. "His family."

The conversation was dredging up more than Chaco had bargained for, and he sensed that if he continued, Pavia might lose what little hold he had on his emotions. Something about this whole Corazon thing was pushing hard at Pavia's pragmatism, which was strange because, when faced with a tough assignment, most corporate soldiers handled things by the book. With Pavia, however, something else was at work, and it seemed to be undermining his professionalism.

They approached an old 12-story building that hadn't seen any retrofitting for at least a decade.

"SATNAV indicates this is the hotel," Chaco said, pointing.

Pavia circled the building twice before he pulled into its parking area. He glided between a cheap CitiCar and a small step-up that had a goofy fish logo on its side. Pavia switched off the car, and its organics hissed into their dormant settings.

Chaco checked his Light-Force and returned it to its holster. He glanced at Pavia, who maintained his grip on the steering toggle and stared at the rain collecting on the windshield. "You a hundred percent with this?" Chaco asked.

Pavia sighed heavily and nodded.

As Chaco stepped into the rain, which was quickly becoming a downpour, his coat's fabric shifted into its protective setting.

"Fucking rain," he heard Pavia say as they trotted towards the hotel's front doors.

The Oprah was typical of the many franchise hotels that

littered New York City. Someone told Chaco once that a famous media giant named Winfrey from earlier in the century had started the chain, but he'd never heard of her. An assortment of extremely used furniture dominated the interior, but it was the overuse of fake wood paneling and brass trim that gave the whole place the feel of a country club for lost souls.

A meticulous, older black gentleman, his face buried in a system screen, looked up from the concierge desk just in time to catch their coats vibrating dry. The white part of his eyes was the color of French vanilla ice cream. They narrowed as Chaco and Pavia approached.

"Gentlemen," he said gravely, "how can I help you this dreary night?" He looked them up and down over a pair of antique reading glasses that worked well with his vintage tweed coat and button-down shirt.

Chaco had retrieved the clerk's stats from the NSA database on the ride over. He clicked open his Netpad and projected his badge along with an enhanced info/image of Marl from the convenience store vid.

The clerk regarded Chaco's ID with little concern.

"Mr. Flossmore," Chaco said in his most official voice, "is this man staying with you?"

The clerk referenced his system, pressing his face inches from the screen. "Yes." He looked to Marl's holoimage and back. "Room 360," he said, tapping the screen with a bony finger. It was missing most of its tip.

"Was this woman with him?" Marl's image dissolved into Corazon's. The clerk studied it intently.

"I can't say that I've seen her, but I usually work days."

Chaco called up the hotel's floor plans. "The stairs are this way," he said to Pavia while pointing at a door to the right of the main elevator banks. As they walked across the lobby, Chaco noticed the carpet looked like it had seen a hundred years of traffic.

"The gov'ment pays for any damages, you know," the clerk called out.

"I know," Chaco said over his shoulder. "Here's the address for any inquiries you might have." He accessed the NSA's PR site and sent it to the hotel's system.

The clerk bent down to view his screen. "All right then," he said, straightening. "You boys be safe." He removed his glasses and let them dangle from a gold chain. "And try and keep it to a minimum, will you please?"

"Minimum, my ass," Pavia said under his breath. He yanked open the exit door, and they began climbing.

The stairwell was cool and emitted a fetid odor, which by the second floor was doing a serious number on Chaco's stomach. His fingers grazed something sticky under the handrail. "Shit, what's that smell?" he asked while he wiped his palm down the side of his pants.

218

"I'll bet you a dinner at Sardi's it's the backside of the all-night buffet." Pavia was now taking two stairs at a time and appeared not the worse for it.

The fire door to the third floor was an old push-latch with the original retrofitted firebox bolted to its frame. The red alarm armature was bent slightly askew to the box like it had been hastily kicked in the past.

"I wonder if it will go off?" Chaco asked.

Pavia reared back and side-kicked the door directly on the armature. The door succumbed and was now hanging by one hinge.

"I was just about to try it," Chaco said. The hallway was barely lit by an exit sign stuck in mid-dissolve between English and Spanish.

"Which way?" Pavia asked.

Chaco referenced his Netpad and pointed. "To the right."

Pavia marched past him, barely navigating the width of the doorframe. Like the stairwell, the hallway's carpet was an aromatic time capsule, and Chaco thought he could pick out various odors. Or maybe there had just been a huge party the night before.

In most New American cities, living space had become a commodity, so the typical hotel crammed as many occupants onto a floor as code would allow. Such was the case with Oprah's in Harlem, and as Chaco followed Pavia down the corridor, muffled room sounds lingered around every door. These audible fragments detached and stuck with Chaco, creating visual scenarios that played out in his mind. Room 309: an argument between two gay guys. Room 312: an old movie, possibly the remake of Superman with that famous black guy in the lead. Room 340: some extreme fucking and spanking. Room 354: a party, but the language was Third World.

"This is it," Pavia said, stepping up to Room 360. Its welcome panel flashed a staticky *La Bienvenida* and cast his face in various shades of electric red.

Chaco drew his Light-Force. Pavia followed, but his was an older model – the kind anyone with connections could get on the Black Net.

"I never saw that," Chaco said, gesturing.

Pavia grunted approvingly, and they waited for the room's system to announce them.

"I don't think it's working," Chaco said.

Pavia rapped his fist against the door. "Marl?!" He waited, then knocked again. "Marl, this is Pavia and Chaco!"

No response.

"This is bullshit." Pavia stepped back and prepped to unleash another kick. Chaco moved to the side of the door and pressed his back against the wall. He wanted to give him a wide berth, but the door buzzed and slid opened.

"Deja?!" Chaco exclaimed. "What the hell?"

"Now listen, Sonny," Deja said, backing up. "Before you

go off, hear me out."

Pavia charged around Chaco into the center of the room. It was deceptively large, and they were standing in a quasi-living room. Off to the left was a hallway that led to a bedroom. The drapes were drawn, and the air felt like the HVAC was on high heat. Deja was standing on the other side of the living room, having backed against a small table. Her palms were up in an appeal for reasonableness and understanding.

"Deja!" Chaco said, holstering his Light-Force, "what are you doing here? I told you to stay out of this. We're not screwing around. This is a serious situation. Corazon's life may be at stake, and we don't know who or what we're dealing with."

"Ms. Moriarty," Pavia said sternly. His Light-Force was still drawn and leveled at her. "Where is Mrs. Goya?"

Chaco stepped up. "You can lower that," he said.

Pavia ignored him, his jaw gnashing fiercely.

"Hey, Pavia, lower the gun. That's an order."

Pavia leaned in, and Chaco noticed that the gun didn't waver. "This isn't your jurisdiction, agent."

Chaco stepped back. "The hell it isn't—"

"Oscar!" Corazon appeared in the hallway that led to the bedroom. Her inflection sounded like she had addressed a family pet that had just lunged at a guest.

"Kita!" Pavia said. He turned without losing his aim on Deja.

"Oscar, dear, I'm all right, see?" Corazon stepped into the

room, her arms spread. "Now put that silly gun away."

Pavia obediently lowered the gun to his side. Chaco, now about five feet from him and completely on edge, removed his Light-Force.

"Are you all right?" Pavia asked, his attention firmly on Corazon.

"Of course, Oscar. Why would I not be?"

"We believe this Marl person may be part of a more organized, global action."

"In a sense, Mr. Pavia, you are correct." Marl emerged from the darkened hallway behind Corazon. In the soft light, Chaco could see he was wearing the same coat as always, but now its pattern was a monochromatic Gaussian noise. It reminded him of the static he had seen on his grandfather's silicon chip-based television when he had flipped through the dead channels.

Pavia slowly raised his gun at Marl.

"I can assure you," Marl continued as he came around Corazon, "this action will be of great significance."

"Step away from her," Pavia said.

"I don't think this is really any of your affair, Oscar."

"Shut the hell up, Marl – or whatever your name is – and step away from her *now*." Pavia engaged the Light-Force's loading sequence; its whine lacerated the tension.

Chaco engaged his own Light-Force, and its sequencer's whine mixed in. He leveled his gun at Pavia.

Marl casually regarded Pavia's Light-Force. A faint smile formed at the edges of his mouth.

"Oscar, please," Corazon pleaded. "For God's sake, Marl is not going to hurt—"

"Kita!" Pavia exclaimed. The sides of his scalp were now moist with sweat. "Please, listen to me. This ... this *clone* is dangerous. Get away from him!"

Corazon stepped back as if by pure reflex.

Marl turned to speak to her. "If you wish to join them, I won't stop you."

Corazon was now about five feet directly behind Marl. Chaco hoped Pavia had sized up the situation's tactical issues.

"Go on," Marl said to Corazon. "It's all right."

Corazon folded her arms and defiantly shook her head.

Pavia raised the Light-Force directly at Marl's chest.

Marl casually considered it and then leveled his attention at Pavia. His look seemed to have the weight of the world behind it, which Chaco was beginning to suspect it might.

"She's made her choice, Oscar," Marl said, his voice an octave lower.

Chaco noticed Pavia's hand was shaking slightly. "Don't do it," he said.

"Fuck it," Pavia replied.

The Light-Force's flash burned the room's features into a violent blur of ball lightning. In the second before Chaco's ocular membranes activated, his brain seemed to seize up, as if what he had just witnessed was too terrible to process.

"My God," he said as the horrific after-image of the Light-Force striking Corazon burned through his conscience.

Dead space

27

CHACO heard, rather than saw, Pavia's gun hit the carpet. The dense weave absorbed much of the noise, though he thought the weapon landed somewhere off his right foot. The room was filled with the sweet smell he remembered from the academy. The floor shook, and he slowly opened his eyes, praying that the negative image burned onto his retinas wasn't real. But as his ocular membranes retracted, he saw that Pavia had dropped to his knees and was sitting on his heels. He had his hands to his mouth and was rocking in sync to what sounded like inhuman moans.

Chaco heard himself say, "Oh no," but he couldn't recall the words actually forming in his mind. Nothing felt quite real, as if he were viewing the whole scene from a distance in a near-death experience, watching himself from above and behind rather than experiencing the scene through his own eyes.

A barking sound edged into his awareness and hovered there, repeating. Gradually, he realized Deja was screaming "Oh, my God," over and over again, but everything came across as one word in quick, sharp gasps.

Their eyes met.

"Sonny ..." she began, but the rest came out in high-pitched squeaks that only captured fragments of the words. He thought she said: What are we going to do?

He looked around, but Marl was gone. The reality of the event punched Chaco in the gut, and his stomach rolled. He walked across the room and took Deja into his arms. She buried her head and cried into his chest. He held her tightly, wishing there was something he could say. She looked up, her cheeks slick with tears.

Chaco began to speak, but stopped himself.

Deja briefly glanced where Corazon had been.

Jesus.

"Sonny, what ..." She couldn't finish.

Chaco had seen the results of a Light-Force discharge on a

lab animal during a training exercise at the academy, but nothing could have prepared him for the debiolization of a human being. He couldn't help but stare at the gelatinous puddle that had been Corazon Kita Goya. It pooled in the threshold of the hallway looking remarkably like a spilled drink. It was hard for him to imagine that, only seconds earlier, it had been a living being. "There's nothing we can do," he said.

"Oh, Cor." Deja broke from his embrace and approached the puddle.

"Don't touch it!" Chaco and his fellow trainees had watched a vid playback of the test firing. Even enhanced slow motion couldn't adequately capture the horror of debiolization, and the residual effects could last for several minutes.

"*Gatito*," Pavia moaned in shock, his arms stretched toward the puddle. Chaco could only feel pity for the man. He walked over and knelt, but Pavia didn't seem to register his presence.

"Oscar," he said softly, "we've got to get out of here. If Marl comes back–"

Pavia whimpered something in a mix of Spanglish and street talk. Chaco could only pick out a few words – "my love" and "little one."

"Oscar," he said more firmly. "We have to get out of here."

Pavia turned and looked at Chaco as if he were dreaming. His eyes were filled with tears, and his hands were trembling.

"Come *on*," Chaco ordered. "You know we have to." The

case was now seriously beyond just fucked up and had entered a very dangerous stage. He looked about again and wondered if Marl would suddenly materialize. What the hell would he do then?

Pavia composed himself and struggled to his feet. Chaco picked up Pavia's gun and handed it to him. Pavia regarded the weapon for a moment before he slipped it under his coat. He glanced at the puddle, and a hardening descended over him, as if another personality had taken over. Chaco figured it was the veteran agent's years of dealing with death that had finally kicked in.

Deja, still squatting by the puddle, mournfully looked up.

"We need to leave now," Chaco said.

"I know," Pavia uttered while he tentatively adjusted his fedora.

"Let's go, Dej," Chaco said.

"Sonny ..." She looked at the puddle and back. "Shouldn't we say a prayer or something?"

He began to agree, but thought better of it. "I don't feel comfortable hanging around. Marl could come back." Chaco didn't really know what to do if Marl returned. His training had never prepared him for a case like this, and he was beginning to think going to someone in DoD maybe wasn't such a bad idea. He felt the stares of Deja and Pavia. "Lets get out of here," he said finally and slipped his gun back into its holster.

"But shouldn't we, ah, clean her up?"

"No! Please don't touch it. It'll be dangerous for at least

another couple of minutes."

Deja quickly backed away from the puddle and drew near Chaco. She wrapped her arm around his waist, and he could feel she was still shaking.

They all gave their attention to the darkening wet spot in the carpet.

"Good bye, Cor," Deja said softly. "I'll miss you."

*   *   *

The Thin's hydoshower didn't seem to be helping. Chaco's gut was all knotted up, and there was a nagging reflux at the back of his throat.

"Increase pressure," he ordered.

The shower responded, and Chaco eagerly accepted its super-heated punches. After 15 minutes, though, he still felt like hell.

"Off!"

He took a towel from its hook and mechanically began drying himself. He was present, but not really. The ride back to The Thin had been silent. Pavia seemed in a daze and didn't even acknowledge Chaco and Deja when they stepped from his car. Chaco's mind kept ebbing back to the after-image of Corazon and what his next moves should be.

"Sonny?" Deja appeared at the bathroom door wrapped in

one of the hotel's lavish bathrobes. Its thick collar cradled her head like angel's wings.

"Yeah?"

She looked at him with such care it almost hurt. "What are you feeling?"

Chaco wrapped the towel around his waist. "To tell you the truth, I'm pretty numb right now." He leaned against the glass hydroshower wall and rubbed what little water was left from his face. "I'm not totally sure what happened. I thought Marl was standing in front of Corazon.... I mean, one second he's there, the next, he's gone? I don't get it. And what the hell was Pavia thinking, firing like that? We have no idea what we're dealing with here. Hitting Marl could have killed all of us!" He cinched the towel tighter. "I don't know what's going on any more. If Marl let this happen, I don't understand the purpose of Corazon's death. And how did he just disappear? That kind of technology doesn't exist. What the *hell* is going on here?!" He stormed past Deja into the bedroom.

She followed. "Maybe Marl had a reason—"

"A reason?!" Chaco stopped in the middle of the room. "What the hell could he possibly gain from letting her die? If he's an alien, he sure as hell didn't come in peace."

Deja settled onto the bed and tucked her knees against her chest. "Maybe he's got a higher purpose," she offered. "One we can't understand."

"You talk like you're defending him. The last time I checked, wasn't Corazon your friend?"

Deja cowered and turned away.

"Oh, baby, I'm sorry." Chaco sat on the bed and tried to comfort her.

Deja leaned back into his hug. "I think she was, Sonny. She was so lonely, and I guess she felt like she could really open up with me."

Chaco held Deja, and for a brief moment the pain of the event was kept at bay.

"What do you think is going to happen to Oscar?" she asked.

"I don't know," he said. "The good news – if there is any – is that since Corazon was illegal, she technically never existed, I mean as a clone. I doubt there's an official death record for the original Kita Goya. So as far as the grid's concerned, she's still living. Goya could just make another clone and let his PR people spin whatever they wanted. But I don't know how Oscar's going to explain the death of Corazon to Goya. I wouldn't want to be in his shoes."

"Sonny ... do you think Oscar was in love with her?"

"I think so. Or at least, he sure reacted like he was."

Deja stared reflectively. "That's so sad."

"Yes, it is. I can't imagine doing–"

Deja squeezed him. "Shh. Don't talk like that."

Chaco kissed her forehead. "Let's get some sleep." He threw the towel to the floor and slid under the covers.

Deja removed her robe and clicked off the light. She nestled into his favorite position: her leg rucked over his waist with her head buried into his shoulder. She felt good – so warm and fresh from her shower – and Chaco had come to love the way her hair smelled. It conjured feelings of security, although he didn't know why.

The room's darkness seemed absolute, and sleep was slow to come. Since Chaco rarely remembered his dreams, sleep was nothing more than the dead space between closing and opening his eyes. Usually, it represented freedom from the stress of working for one of the world's most powerful organizations. Tonight was different, however. All he could feel was a predacious fear lurking near the boundary of his soul. He gently squeezed Deja, and she moaned softly.

"Dear God," he whispered into the room's void, "please don't let me dream tonight."

Bullshit

"**YOU** want another hit, honey?"

Gives-a-Crap shifted the tray to her other hand. Her t-shirt this morning was promotional swag for an L.A. band named Thickboys. Their tattooed heads appeared too big for their bodies; their necks looked like blobs of solder from a bad welding job. It wasn't a bioshirt, which was a relief to Deja. If a place had more than a dozen people wearing them in a small space – such as Bar of Soap – it could get real old, real fast. She just wasn't up for that in-your-face crap this early ... especially *this* morning.

"Hmm?" Deja belatedly replied, glancing up from her Netpad.

"Do you want another one?" Gives-a-Crap was pointing at Deja's empty coffee cup.

"Ah, no. I'm fine." Deja resumed her news scan, but so far there was no mention of anything unusual at a hotel in Harlem.

"What's the matter? Rough night?"

Deja looked up again, wanting nothing more than to be alone. "You could say that."

"Me, too. I got so wasted I don't remember half of it. How 'bout you?"

"I wish I could forget all of it."

"Been there." Gives-a-Crap moved on to a trashed four top of club kids near the dryers. Earlier, Deja had watched them out of the corner of her eye as they wolfed down their breakfasts. Judging by appearances, they had raged all night, and when Deja walked to the bathroom, the faint smell of honey confirmed they were heavy Riders. Not to mention the tiny metal doors they had pierced in their shoulders. That's where they injected their Jack. The sight of them made her skin crawl.

Deja put down her Netpad by the plate of miniature bread samples and resumed pushing her oatmeal around. She had already blended its milk and brown sugar into a fine paste that resembled the wall putty she had used to patch her old apartment in Miami. She made a half-hearted attempt to eat.

"So, where's your better half?" Gives-a-Crap asked, sliding up to the table. Her tray was loaded with the carnage of the club kids' breakfasts.

"He had a rough night, too, so I let him sleep in. He kind of deserved it."

"I think men would sleep all day if we let them."

Deja politely nodded at this viscid declaration and pretended to resume eating.

"Well, I'll leave you to your breakfast." Gives-a-Crap turned and sauntered toward the counter, balancing the loaded tray deftly on her fingertips.

Deja picked up the Netpad, logged into the New York Times lifestyle section, and dutifully swallowed some oatmeal. Skimming the articles, her attention landed on a fashion segment highlighting the new fall collections from Paris. She intently studied the pictorial and tried to lose herself in the images, but the previous night's horror wouldn't let go. Deja wished her mind could become as vacuous as the models' expressions. She unconsciously took another spoonful of oatmeal. A gust of cool air passed through the booth.

"May I join you?"

Deja looked up with a start and almost choked.

Marl was standing beside her booth. He had on the same coat – its pattern calm – and sported his stupid smile, which Deja would have slapped off his face if it weren't for the fear that had seized her. She sank into the booth as far as she could go.

"What do you want?" she asked suspiciously.

"To join you. May I?"

"Would it matter if I said no?"

"It would, but I know you won't. You want answers, don't you?"

Deja felt an odd mix of fear and anger towards Marl. Here, sitting across from her and looking like nobody special, was possibly the planet's first true "close encounter." But he also was the cause of Corazon's death. Although Deja felt she should be freaking in his presence, all that filled her was an intense hatred. She angrily folded her arms as Marl slid into the booth.

"You got some galactic balls coming in here," she said.

Marl cocked his head like he didn't get her meaning.

"What kind of insane world do you come from, and how could you let Cor be killed?" Deja felt her voice rising, but she didn't care.

Marl's face went blank. "It was unfortunate that–"

"Unfortunate?! *Unfortunate*? If I had a Light-Force, I'd reduce you to a puddle of bio crap. Then we'd see who be–"

"I need to speak with you, but not like this." Marl's tone was even, calculated.

Fuming, Deja leaned onto the table. "Why should I?"

"Because," Marl said, "you need to understand."

"The only thing I need is to get the hell away from—"

"Find the best Virtgear you can, and meet me in the same NSA Net conference room where I met Mr. Tsukahara. And let's not tell Sonny."

Deja clenched her fists. "What if I don't want to?"

"I *know* you do."

"And just how will I find that kind of Virtgear?"

"You'll know how," Marl said flatly, and the dumb-ass grin returned. "Be there in three hours."

"Honey?" Deja remotely registered off to her right. The sound repeated.

Gives-a-Crap was standing at the opening to the booth, her hands on her wide hips. "Who the 'H' are you talking to?" Two other people stood behind her, each with their laundry baskets tucked under their arms. They were craning around Gives-a-Crap.

"Huh?" Deja said, disoriented. Suddenly she felt nauseous, like the time she had done VirtScape when her boyfriend had altered the program. She had materialized high over the Grand Canyon and almost thrown up inside her face gear.

"Girl, you were chatting up a storm," Gives-a-Crap said. "And by the sound of it, you were in some kind of argument. Are you all right?"

The other side of the booth was empty. "Yeah," Deja replied.

Gives-a-Crap nodded. "Well, if you need anything – like

an extra coffee for your friend – just yell." She laughed and walked away. The two others looked Deja over, shrugged to each other, and followed Gives-a-Crap to the counter.

Deja's heart rate couldn't quite return to normal, although she was regaining the ability to think. Her better self said to run back and wake Chaco up. But for some strange reason, Deja still couldn't overcome the feeling that Marl's intentions were probably for the better. Even though it was killing her to have Cor gone, she couldn't deny that her death might have played a part in Marl's "master plan" to fix the world. Maybe if she did go in and meet with Marl, she'd be able to find out what he was going to do. And if it was something terrible, she could warn Sonny. The more she thought about, the more Deja felt that it was her duty to meet with Marl. And when did she ever listen to her better self anyway? She picked up her Netpad and entered a number.

"Who the hell is calling me this early?" The image on the Netpad's tiny screen jumped in frames, like the person answering was using an old style vidphone.

"Bartas? It's me, Deja. From the other night?"

"Oh, yes, Oscar's friend. How could I forget such a pretty face? What can I do for you at this ungodly hour?"

She hesitated. "I need your help."

*   *   *

"I haven't heard from Oscar since you were here," Bartas said while he led Deja down the hallway to the room filled with Netgear. He coughed. "Did you ever find that woman you were looking for, the one Oscar lost?"

"Yes," Deja said.

"How did it go?"

"Not well."

"Oh, I'm sorry to hear that." He coughed again, this time a series of hacks that almost made Deja's ribs hurt. "I trust nothing bad happened," he said, recovering.

Deja shrugged, hoping he'd stop with the questions. He did, and led her into the room.

"Okay," Bartas said and folded his arms. "Why do you want to go in?" The robe had short sleeves, and Deja could see that there was barely enough muscle on his arms for them to function. They reminded her of the puny chicken wings floating in the egg broth at Kim's buffet on 8th.

"Because, ah, Sonny wants to meet and show me something."

"And why do you need to use my Virtgear?"

"Because I want to surprise Sonny. It's kind of ... personal."

Bartas looked Deja over in a way that made her feel uncomfortable. She was used to guys checking her out, but Bartas's gaze lingered a little too long on her breasts, and he had an air about him that went beyond sexual. "Really?" he said. "You two aren't, you know, going to one of those sex sites are you? You understand your boyfriend won't have the same sensations you will."

"Ah, well ... it's not quite like that," Deja said. "Sonny wants me to meet him in the NSA conference room."

"You mean the one where we were last time?"

Deja nodded, not really knowing what to say next.

"I don't want to know," Bartas said. "You've come all this way, so it must be pretty important. Besides, I'm up, and I've got nothing better to do. I'm always a sucker for this kind of crap. Come on. Hop up here, and we'll get you hooked up. I still have the coordinates in my system." He patted the virt chair Chaco had used.

Deja tentatively climbed up and settled back.

"Have you used Virtual High Density much?"

"Oh, yeah," Deja lied.

"Well, this is like VHD, but on steroids." Bartas laughed and stepped over to the control console. He fiddled with a few interface pads. "Okay, that should do it. Now, sit back and just relax. Remember, the more you fight, the harder it grabs."

Deja settled against the cool biofabric. Its organics quivered beneath her like a trillion fingertips until the chair had completely processed her body's shape.

Bartas sat at the console and picked up a handheld Virtgear unit.

"Are you going in with me?" Deja asked, alarmed.

"Hell yes. You think I'd let a novice jump up on my

equipment and ride in alone? Believe me, it's nothing I've never seen before."

"I said this is kind of personal."

"You want in or not?"

"Fine. We'll do it your way. But remember, this is between Sonny and me. If you do anything–"

"Easy, young lady. I'm old enough to be your daddy. Besides, with my condition, a hurricane couldn't get me up. Just go and have a good time, or whatever you want to do. I'll set it just to monitor your vitals. I won't have any sensory presence."

For some reason, Deja didn't quite believe him.

Bartas spun back to the console. "On my mark."

Deja closed her eyes and sucked in a deep breath.

"Three, two, one," he said, and the chair attacked her.

Deja had done the cyberspace thing before (who hadn't?), but never like this. All of her senses were working with an amplification that bordered on painful. She ran her fingers across the top of the NSA conference table.

"Different, isn't it?" said a voice inside her head.

Deja quickly surveyed the room. "Bartas?"

"Who'd you think it was?"

"This is amazing," she said, inspecting the various surfaces. "How did you come up with this?"

"I've had a lot of time on my hands lately, if you know what

I mean."

"You should patent this. You'd be rich."

"That's the idea."

Deja picked up a pitcher of water and a glass from a credenza. She filled the glass and tentatively raised it to her lips.

"Go ahead," Bartas urged.

She did. "Oh, my God. It's like I really swallowed the water!"

Bartas laughed and then began coughing.

"You okay?"

"Don't mind me. I'm going to exit here, but I'll still be in the system monitoring your vitals. I can't see or hear you, so you two can do your thing ... or whatever you want to do."

"Thanks, Bartas. I owe you one."

"No, you don't." He hacked. "I'm just glad to see someone using the chair. Enjoy yourself." His coughing faded from her mind.

Deja walked to the opposite side of the room and studied a landscape painting. Its colors of a French countryside were so vibrant the oil seemed be crawling across the canvas.

"Hello."

Deja turned and found Marl at the head of the conference table. She defiantly folded her arms. "So ... I'm here. Now what?"

Marl's coat was rippling with the hues of the Caribbean Sea. She had been once, years ago, to this island – Tortilla something – with a guy she had met through CeCe. He was tall and lean and had flaming red hair, which at the time Deja had found sexy. He worked in the government but never mentioned which branch, and when she had pressed for an answer, he'd just smiled like he was about to sell her a used car. The place where they had stayed was right on the water.

"Thank you" Marl said, his voice having the same flatness as it had at Bar of Soap. "I know this was difficult for you on such short notice." His coat seemed in cadence with his speech. It was a strange effect, and if Deja looked at it long enough, she became a little queasy. "You're here," he continued, "because you want to understand why I let Corazon perish."

Deja nodded angrily.

"This may be hard for you to comprehend."

"Try me."

"It's imperative that I understand what Sonny's assistant calls the 'chi' of your world, in order to heal it."

"You've lost me a little."

"Chi, Deja, is a very appropriate word in this context. It's the Chinese name for the vital force that enlivens all matter – the pre-atomic constructs of energy."

"Get to the point."

"In order to understand your world, I have to understand what drives its people." Marl began to slowly walk around the large table. "And what drives humans are their emotions. No matter their race, culture, or socioeconomic level, all humans base their decisions around their emotional point of view. Why do you think your planet is in such a state? Essentially, your world's emotions are out of balance."

An image of Corazon laughing at the bar at Desperate Sense flashed across Deja's mind. "Yeah, but I still don't understand why you had to let Cor die."

Marl stopped at a table with a vase of gladiolas on it. He passed a finger along a leaf. "Grief," he said as if it pained him to state the obvious. His coat flared slightly.

"What are you talking about?"

"Grief, along with anger, sadness, shame. Death harbors a whole host of emotions for your species, and I had to experience them."

"But did you have to let her die?" Deja asked. "Couldn't you have just done that thing you do, you know, make it happen in our minds, instead of for real?" She felt tears welling in the corners of her eyes.

"No," Marl said coldly.

"Bullshit."

Marl thought for a moment. "I needed genuineness."

"You got that!"

Marl resumed walking. "Corazon was special. Her view of the world was unique. She was the crucial link for me to understand the most important emotion on your planet."

"Which one?"

"Love." Marl stopped again and smiled, but not his usual

stupid grin. Deja felt this one came from his soul, if he had one.

"So now you're telling me you *loved* her?" Deja was growing suspicious.

"Not in the sense that you'd understand." Marl started pacing again. "I've experienced most of the emotional states that can be reached by your species. And with Corazon, I reached a level of understanding that I believe only a few on your planet ever achieve. But we lacked a certain ... element." He stopped one chair from her, and his gaze washed over her chest.

Deja took a step back and bumped against the credenza. The water sloshed in the pitcher, and her stomach felt like it had tightened into a knot the size of a baseball. "W-what element is that?"

Marl's eyes narrowed. "Lust."

Bucket of assholes

29

CHACO rolled over, and his head slid off the pillow. He groped for Deja through the dark.

"Dej?"

The only sound that returned was his own blood coursing through his ears. He glanced at the clock. *8:35 a.m.*

"Shit," he said under his breath. "Deja?!"

Nothing.

"Question."

"Yes, how may I help you?" asked the room's HDI system.

"Is the guest, Deja Moriarty, in the hotel?"

A pause. "The guest, Deja Moriarty, is not in the hotel. She left the property at approximately 5:32 a.m. this morning."

Chaco sat up. He swung his legs over the side of the bed and rubbed his face. *Goddamn it*. He grabbed his coat off the chair by the bed and pulled out his Netpad. He punched in a number sequence. Yoichi Tsukahara's face pixeled up. He was in their NSA lab and appeared to be alone.

"Yes, Chacosan?"

"Tsuka, I need for you to find Deja Moriarty on the grid. Her ID code will be in the Goya case file. Access it through the internal network using the password M-I-M-I."

"Yes, sir." Chaco watched Tsukahara roll to a console and scan through the system. The time it took was killing him.

"Tsuka, let's hustle it up."

Tsukahara quickly rolled back. "She's in the state of New Jersey, sir, at 439 North Adams–"

"That's okay, I know the address." He thought for a second. "I need you to meet me in one of the NSA's Net conference rooms. Use the same coordinates we used before."

Tsukahara bowed.

"And, hey, Tsuka. This is *really* important, understand?"

"Yes, sir!" He bowed deeper.

Chaco tapped in another number, and the face of Oscar

Pavia filled the screen. He didn't respond.

"Did I catch you at a bad time?" Chaco asked.

"Time is what I have a lot of now." Pavia's attention was focused on something he was doing out of the camera's view field.

"Why's that?"

"I've joined the ranks of the unemployed."

"Sorry to hear that. How did it go down with Goya?"

"As expected."

"What did you finally end up telling him?"

"Not the truth. I wouldn't be speaking to you if I had." Pavia walked away from the screen and into a small living room. He picked up a glass of orange juice from a circular coffee table and returned. His mass distorted at edges of the screen. He finally faced the camera. "Goya's in Mexico City. I told him that Corazon died in an attempted kidnapping. Crossfire accident, you know. In my business, extortion is a way of life. I blamed it on one of the cartels. Goya's got so many enemies it could be any one of a dozen factions. My replacement is working on finding out who did it. He'll be fucking with that for months, and by then I'll be long gone from this shit-hole country. Goya wasn't too broken up about it. I guess he figures he can make himself another one, probably better this time."

"Hey, Oscar?"

"Yeah?"

"I think Deja's with your brother."

Pavia's drink stopped short of his mouth; he frowned over the edge of the glass. "Why?"

"If I had to guess ... Marl."

Pavia shook his head. "What is she doing?"

"Something stupid, that's for sure. I gotta get down there, and I was hoping you'd join me."

Pavia set the drink aside. "You go. I've got to take care of something."

"Oscar, don't go after Marl."

"I have to, Sonny."

"Look, I think I know how you felt for Corazon, but—"

Pavia shot him a look.

"Okay, maybe I don't. But I do know that this Marl thing is in another league. I'm still not sure what happened. He must have been holoprojecting or something. And I can't get my head around why he did what he did. What was there to gain?"

"I think it was about me."

"What? That's absurd."

"Sonny, I've made a lot of enemies over the years."

"No, if that were the case, why did he approach Deja with that bizarre alien story?"

"You don't understand. The people I have dealt with are ruthless. Cross them, and they'll jack with you from all angles. They'll even kill the family of your brother if they thought it would get to you ... psychologically."

This last statement sent a shiver through Chaco. His mind flashed on the file of Bartas's family. "No," Chaco said, shaking his head, "I don't think it's like that. This clone is way beyond anything I've ever seen or studied. Whatever he is, I'm beginning to consider Tsuka's story."

"Sonny, come on—"

"No, I mean it. Something's not right here."

"Look, I don't really care what he – or it – is. All I know is that I have to defend Corazon's memory. It's my nature."

Chaco sighed. "Watch yourself. We have no idea what we're getting into. By the time I get to Bartas's, this situation could be a real bucket of assholes."

Pavia chuckled.

"What?" Chaco asked, suddenly realizing he had been nervously pulling at the patch of hair below his lip.

"Nothing. My father used to use that phrase. It just made me think."

"My dad did, too."

Both men studied each other.

"You be careful, Sonny," Pavia said.

Chaco took another pull. "You, too. I've got a bad feeling about this."

Something for Lao-Tzu to ponder

30

"**IF** you know so much about us, then you know that in my culture, we have a little thing called morals," Deja said, edging down the credenza.

"You wouldn't give of yourself to save your planet?" Marl asked, stepping closer.

Deja stopped and put her hands up. "All right, that's it. Bartas!"

"He won't be able to help you."

Deja's nerves spiked. "Listen, Marl," she said while she sidestepped a chair, "I'd be the first to help our screwed-up world, but I've got my limits."

Tsukahara's image suddenly formed on the other side of the table.

"Yoichi!" Deja exclaimed.

"Ms. Moriarty," he said surprised, and bowed.

Deja ran around the table and came up to Tsukahara. She mouthed "That's him."

"Pardon?" Tsukahara asked.

Marl said something to Tsukahara in what Deja thought was Japanese. Tsukahara responded, and they conversed for a moment.

Deja looked from Tsukahara to Marl. "Hey, what are you two saying?"

"I was just telling Yoichi how good it was to finally meet him ... face-to-face," Marl said.

"Ms. Moriarty," Tsukahara began. "Marl is the presence I told Agent Chaco about. The one who spoke to me ... about certain things ... in my thoughts."

"Yeah," Deja said, "he has a way of doing that."

"Yoichi knows all about my mission," Marl said, "and he probably knows better than most how screwed up," his eyes moved to Deja, "this world can be. Don't you, Yoichi?"

Tsukahara averted Marl's gaze and nodded.

Marl suddenly approached Tsukahara, passing Deja like she didn't exist. He stopped about two feet in front him, and Deja could see an immense discrepancy between their virtual forms. Tsukahara looked like an ancient video signal compared to Marl's perfection. The difference was shocking.

"Curious," Marl said, studying Tsukahara's pixilated form. "Often, your species is at its best when it's at its worst. Something for Lao-Tzu to ponder, eh, Yoichi?" He took a step back. "It was good to speak with you again. I hope we talk soon."

Tsukahara shot a startled look at Deja and began to protest, but his image de-pixeled and was gone.

"Now," Marl said, turning, "weren't you about to help your planet?"

Interesting  31

"I didn't think I'd hear from you again, agent. You know this ride is gonna cost you a bundle."

"I know," Chaco said, watching the gray mass of buildings that canyoned the Interway blur by the passenger window.

The cab driver glanced back over the half-raised plexi. "You're lucky to catch me this early. I usually get off around seven." He looked again. "What's eatin' you?"

"Got a lot on my mind."

"I never heard from you after I dropped you off at Heaven. What happened to that girl you was tailin'?"

"That night got a little, ah ... complex."

"I hope it was good complex."

"It wasn't."

"That sucks." The driver returned his attention to the road.

*   *   *

"This is it. Want me to wait for ya?"

"Yeah," Chaco said, "but it might take a while."

"Don't worry. I still got your card in my system." The cab driver looked out the windshield at the rows of storage units. "Who the hell would live in one of these?"

"Nobody you'd want to know."

A light rain was falling as Chaco approached Bartas's front door. He pressed the buzzer and waited. No answer. He tried again. Still nothing. Finally, he called up the NSA's field program for residential security systems and held his Netpad to the face of the lock. Still no response. It was an old palm-print lock that apparently would take a few passes for the program to find Bartas's records and reproduce the digital code for the lock's hard drive to recognize. After a fourth pass, it clicked, and the deadbolts released. The porch light flickered.

Chaco slowly opened the door and was hit with that sick

smell, but it was even more pungent now. The repeated failed calls to Bartas made him suspicious, and his guard was about to go through the roof. He cautiously edged through the maze of boxes that crowded the front door.

"Hello? Bartas? Deja?"

Silence.

Chaco removed his Light-Force and crept down the dark hallway towards the Net room. At the Academy, he always had trouble with interior tactical simulations. Something about the restricted movement made it hard for him to concentrate. His thoughts began to wander to Bartas, his sickness, and his dead family.

Come on. Concentrate.

Chaco edged up to the open doorway of the Net room and put his back against the wall. He engaged the Light-Force's sequencer and held the weapon loosely, as he had been trained. If he gripped it too tightly, it might go off if he got spooked. And right now, he was pretty fucking spooked. He slowly peeked around the doorframe and saw Bartas slumped in a chair at the main console. He was wearing a different robe than before, and his head was wrapped in a standard Virtgear unit. White spittle clung to the corners of his mouth. He looked dead, except one of his arms hung down the side of the chair, and his fingers were twitching. Even that didn't mean much. If a person died while virt-in, the neuro-connections would continue to feed a signal that could cause muscles to twitch.

Chaco fully entered the room and spotted Deja in Bartas's VirtChair. Her body was entwined with connector tentacles, and her fists were clenched as if she were in some kind of pain. He noticed a large wet spot at her crotch, which was easy to see thanks to her bright green lycra shorts that he liked so much. Chaco had learned that people rarely pissed their pants when they were virt-in, but Bartas's chair made the experience hyper-real, and according to the manuals, people only pissed when they were scared out of their wits.

Bartas's pulse was low but steady, and he reeked of sickness. Chaco inspected the console and saw that the conference room actually had three occupants: Bartas, Deja, and an "unknown," but the readings for the unknown weren't in a range that would define life.

Deja groaned and arched her back. Chaco approached the chair and reached for one of the tentacles, which reacted by tightening around her arm. He desperately wanted to help Deja, but a radical separation from Virtgear might kill her. He didn't know enough about Bartas's chair to risk that. The only way to help her was to get into the Net meeting room. Chaco searched for another Virtgear unit but couldn't find one. He walked back to Bartas and eyed his unit.

"Sorry man," he said and gripped the unit by its main body. Its tentacles quivered. He began to pull, but the unit clamped tighter around Bartas's head.

Deja groaned again.

Chaco yanked with all of his weight, and the unit slipped off, leaving behind a series of ugly scratches on Bartas's face and neck. When the last tentacle broke free, they all retracted into the housing. Bartas's head snapped back, and his chair rolled into a computer stack. The impact knocked Bartas forward. He landed on the floor in a crumpled heap.

Chaco pulled the chair over and sat at the console. Bartas's conference room marker was gone, leaving Deja's and the unknown's.

"Shit," he said and slapped the Virtgear unit to his forehead.

As Chaco's vision faded in, he was greeted by an uncompromisingly blinding radiance that burned away much of the conference room's detail. Virtual reality had a way of tricking the mind, especially when it came to pain, and he thought he felt his ocular membranes automatically close. Peering through the glare, he could barely make out Deja and Marl. They were across the room at the end of the conference table, and Marl's coat was glowing like a small sun. Deja had her back to Chaco and was in silhouette. It took him a second to realize she was completely naked.

Marl was standing in front of her. In the glow, Chaco could only make out parts of his face. His eyes were closed, and his hand was pressed against the center of Deja's chest. The whole scene made something boil over in Chaco – a primitive need to protect, but driven by hate. He tried to lunge towards them, but something prevented his lower body from working.

"Get away from her!" he yelled, fighting the force that trapped him.

Marl didn't respond.

"Get the *hell* away from her!"

Marl remained silent, but the glow from his coat appeared to flare slightly.

"I swear to God, if you hurt her in any way, I'll kill you!"

Marl removed his hand, and Deja collapsed into one of the tall, black conference chairs. It slowly turned, and Chaco gasped.

With one arm caught behind her like a rag doll, Deja looked like a victim from one of the vids Chaco had seen in his Intro to Homicide class. She had the freakish expression of one whose last moments were filled with terror: the eyes wide with fear, and the blank stare of death. A dark handprint between her breasts stood out like an old-fashioned brand. The light from Marl's coat instantly vanished; the room regained its normal level of detail.

"Goddamn it, you fucking son-of-a-bitch!" Chaco screamed.

Expressionless, Marl slowly opened his eyes.

"I'll kill you. I swear, as long as it takes me, I'll find a way!"

"Sonny," Marl said calmly as he began walking toward him around the table, "this is only her virtual form." He stopped and passed his hand across Deja's hair before he continued towards Chaco. "She'll be all right. A little sore maybe, but she's a strong woman."

Chaco felt himself dangerously close to the edge of his sanity. "Fuck!" he exclaimed, spittle flying. He struggled against the invisible bands that held him. "If we were in the real world, I'd reduce you to a fucking puddle!"

Marl stopped within inches of Chaco's face and began studying him like a rare piece of art. The detail in Marl's virtual form was astonishing; it reminded Chaco of the first time he had ever witnessed Alto Definition: no pixel gradation, just a continuous image that appeared wherever the targeting gun beamed it.

Marl leaned closer. "You truly want to kill me," he said. "You're so filled with hate that the emotion has taken over some of your higher brain functions." He raised his hand to Chaco's chest. "I *have* to experience this."

The instant Marl's fingertips contacted Chaco's pixeled form, the conference room fell away. He found himself standing on the stairs of his parent's old mobile home, facing their yard filled with abandoned cars his dad planned to someday strip down for their organics. It never happened. His mother had finally sold them to the strange bearded guy who lived on the other side of the transport park. That man had given Chaco the heeby-jeebies,

always looking at his mom funny, like he wanted to date her or
something. After his dad had died, the man had come around
often and said really stupid things like how a boy should have a man
to look up to. As if Chaco would have ever looked up to an asshole
like him. The guy had shot himself a year later, making love to
Mister Sixteen-gauge after an evening of binge drinking. But that
was western Oklahoma at its trashiest, and it took the Marine Corps
to get Chaco the hell out of there.

The sun was setting, and the sky was filled with brilliant
amber striations created by hard-blowing wind and red clay. Chaco
missed sunsets on the plains. They had a sensibility you could
taste. But if anyone ever asked him where he was from, he always
said Tulsa. Who the hell wanted to be from a place called Hooker?

The screen door opened behind him. Anywhere else, that
sound wouldn't mean much, but here in the callused hell lovingly
referred to as the Panhandle, it usually meant that class was in
session, and his dad – flush with Jack and stoked as a Banty rooster
– was preparing another lesson on the hard life to his only son. Chaco
felt the hairs on his arms rise in what his grandmother used to call
goose pimples, though he never understood exactly what the phrase
meant. He instinctually flinched and turned.

"Hello, Sonny," Marl said from the top step. He let go of
the door, and it shut with a crack.

Chaco stepped off the last stair and backed into the middle
of the yard, or what his parents had called a yard. In reality, it was

an encrusted patch of caliche-stained earth that was home to three early BioBugs and a late-model ethanol burner. Dust kicked around his feet, which he noticed were donned with the last pair of Tony Lamas he'd ever owned. He had on the jeans and shirt he had bought with that cute waitress. God, he had loved her.

"Good to be home?" Marl asked. He stepped down one stair.

Chaco looked about and caught the punch of a dry wind against the side of his face. His hair whipped across his eyes.

Hair?

He quickly felt his head and ran his fingers through the shoulder-length mane he wore just before he had shipped out to boot camp.

Marl stepped off the last stair and approached, keeping what Chaco took as a calculated distance.

For an instant, Chaco had been back home, but he quickly shook off the illusion. He could make a go for Marl's throat, maybe even kill his virtual form. But what would that do? "Cut the shit, Marl," he said, folding his arms. "What's this all about? What the hell did you do to Deja?"

Marl gave him the same heavy look again. "This is your memory, Sonny. Why are we here?"

"I don't know." Chaco studied the scene, and suddenly he was 18 again. A thickness rose in his throat, and he tasted the dust and sweat of his youth.

And of a life he thought he had forgotten.

"What's the matter, Sonny? Is this not where you wanted to be?" Marl was leaning against one of the BioBugs. His coat was calm, its stitch pattern as inert as the soil beneath their feet.

"I just hadn't thought much about this place for a long time," Chaco said.

"Why?"

"Don't fuck with me like this. What have you done to Deja?"

Marl smiled. "I would never do anything to harm her, Sonny. When she wakes, she'll have no memory of our time in the conference room."

"You scared the shit out of her. What were you doing to her ... some kind of mind rape?" Chaco felt his anger rising again.

"That was the point. Her emotion was base, primitive. For her, only the fear of rape could bring forth such a raw emotional response. Fear is your species' second most powerful emotion – and the driving force behind many of your culture's most important decisions. I now can also state conclusively that it's one of the most destructive."

"What's the first?"

Marl stood motionless while the wind flapped the front of his coat. "Rage," he said finally.

Another gust of dry air brought a protesting creak from the screen door. Chaco flinched again.

Marl's eyes moved to the door. "Bad memories?"

"You could say that."

Marl regarded Chaco, but the heavy look was gone. "You fascinate me, Sonny. In you, I have found the dichotomy that represents man at his essence."

"Excuse me?" For a second, Chaco had to search his memory for the meaning of "dichotomy."

"You, like mankind, struggle every day with your rational and primal natures."

"That's pretty lame psychology coming from a superior race."

Marl smiled. "I'll grant you it's not – oh, what's the phrase – an earth-shattering discovery. But you have to admit, Sonny, you are an excellent example. You have learned to control your primal side, but not completely. When pushed, as with the perceived rape of Deja, your emotional state spins out of balance. Your primal drive intrudes on your brain's higher functions; your rational control breaks down; and you descend into a blinding rage." He stepped away from the BioBug and leveled that look again. "One that can *kill*." The screen door creaked again, and Marl's eyes went to it. "Like father, like son?"

"Shut the fuck up." The door creaked again. Chaco covered his ears and closed his eyes. "Damn it, stop that wind!"

The wind ebbed. Chacho slowly opened his eyes and found Marl directly in front of him.

"Don't worry, Sonny," he said. "You'll never be as violent as your father was."

Chaco looked away and wiped a tear from the corner of his eye. *Just that last gust of wind*, he thought.

Marl placed a hand on his shoulder. "It's not the wind, Sonny."

Chaco shrugged off the gesture. "I've already been in therapy," he said. "Why did you let Corazon die?"

"To experience what you call death."

"How can you justify your actions like that?"

"She can be made again."

Suddenly the blackness of Marl's coat grew so dense it hid any indications of folds or creases. For a second, Chaco lost any sense of its surface, as if it had no depth or dimensional form. Then, as if from inside it, a million little white specs pulsed and faded. They had flared so quickly that all Chaco could make out were random patterns peppered with tiny clusters. It all looked so familiar. Then it clicked.

Space.

"Why are we really here?" Marl asked, his voice now melodic and sounding like one those aboriginal Australian horns.

Chaco threw his attention to the dirt. "I don't know," he said, following the stitch pattern across the red tips of his Tony Lamas. "Because this is where I'm from?"

"This place," Marl motioned to the mobile home and the

yard, "makes up the core of your true self … the foundation of your nature. Like you, your species has become so preoccupied with commerce that it's forgotten where its home is."

Chaco cautiously looked up and met the alien's eyes. Their color shifted in a thixotropic movement that seemed in sync with the clouds. "What are you, Marl?" he asked. "Why have you come?"

The smile that etched Marl's face reminded Chaco of his father's – before the hard life began. "I find it curious," he said, "that all of your religions, even atheism, share two common fundamentals: to respect one another, and to help one another. Don't you think it's about time your world started putting these concepts into practice?"

"You haven't answered my questions."

"Where I'm from is really irrelevant, Sonny, because in my estimation, it'll be centuries before your species makes it past your own solar system. To your question of 'what are you?' you could say I'm a projector."

Chaco remembered the stupid machine his grandfather used to drag out of the closet every Christmas to make him and his cousins watch old vids called "home movies," which was strange since there was never a home in any of them. His dad had called the machine a projector. "I-I don't understand," he said.

"I project my being, my … true self. That's one way we communicate. My original form projected to your world, then that form expanded across the collective consciousness. It's difficult to translate. We used to be like you."

"But I see you in reality. Physically, I mean."

"You see me, Sonny, with your mind, not your eyes."

Chaco flashed on another memory of a weird neighbor in the transport park. She was one of those fringe "MacLainians," always trying to convert his mom. She would go on and on about how she could look into a person's eyes and tell if they were going to have cancer or something. When he was older, his mom explained that this lady's religion had taken a 20th-century actress as their prophet, but now he was remembering how this lady always talked about her travels, and how his mom tried to explain it wasn't to places like Guymon, or Alva, or even Dallas. This lady's spirit was traveling. She called it a couple of different things. One was soul travel, and the other was astral something, but he couldn't remember. "Are you talking about soul travel?" he asked.

Marl stood there thinking, but Chaco suspected it was more like processing. "Not really," he said finally, "but that's probably the best description your culture would possess."

"You still haven't answered my last question."

"I believe I'm here," Marl said, his voice now soft and liquid-like, "to remind your species where their home is."

At that, an omnipresent calm settled around Chaco and Marl. It deadened all sound and rendered the landscape a monochromatic canvas of grays and blues. Marl's face became questioning, as if he had suddenly forgotten something.

"What's wrong?" Chaco asked. He figured it was unlikely a creature like Marl actually had the capacity to forget.

Marl stared at the dying sunset, his attention apparently consumed with whatever had invaded his mind. "Interesting," he said to himself.

"What's that?"

Marl slowly brought his gaze around. His eyes glowed the color of magma. "It appears," he said, his voice harmonizing with the wind that had kicked up, "that Mr. Pavia has just entered my hotel room."

And the next  32

THROUGH the angular darkness he senses the hatred, guttural and abraded, as it overflows into the room like floodwaters from an unholy river.

Marl opens his eyes.

The 30-million candlepower spotlight of a police gunship cuts a narrow path across the wall. The familiar droning of the craft's rotors follow as it passes above the building on its nightly flyover. The beam traverses the room and catches the edge of a hat's brim, traces the contours of an arm, and reveals just a hint of a figure's threatening mass. It quickly passes over the silhouette of a gun, whose chrome muzzle winks before the beam vanishes. The room is black again.

There is an explosion of light, seemingly brighter than the combined luminosity of his world's twin suns. He senses the air expand as the weapon sends trillions of photons, each laden with matter-altering death, down a super-heated beam that consumes the distance to impact at 299 thousand meters per second.

He feels for the thread count and screams.

*   *   *

The maid stands at Room 360's only window and greets the sun for the first time that day. The ashen clouds that hung over the city only hours earlier have dissipated to reveal a brilliant sunrise. The room's Netscreen displays the day's forecast: a low-pressure front is moving down from the Canadian boarder, and the expected high temperature is 64 degrees.

Behind her, the cleaning cart goes about its duties, moving through the room with a systematic precision. She listens to its sounds as it methodically cleans every surface: the squeak of the dry towel across the glass of the unused shower, the low industrial hum of its vacuum head, the hiss of the toilet's disposal jets cycling. Finally, there is a rush of water as it refills the decanter.

She collects her things and solemnly follows the cart as it automatically departs the suite, a ritual she has repeated for over 30 years.

On to the next room.

And the next.

She never questions the odd smell, or the large stain in the carpet where the bed had stood.

I'm a strong girl  33

DEJA woke to a vicious headache carving its way into the canals of her teeth. She gingerly lifted her head from the pillow and opened her eyes. The dull red glow from the bedside table read 2:34 a.m.

"Hey," she heard out of the room's twilight. The voice seemed distant.

She tried to speak but found this sent the pounding in her head into an unbearable cycle.

"Don't try," she heard.

A dark, blurred form sat on the bed and placed something cool and moist to her forehead. "How many fingers am I holding up?" It sounded like something Chaco would say.

She could only make out the bulbous silhouette of a hand. She limply raised two fingers.

"Good. Now this is going to sting a little, but in about 60 seconds you'll begin feeling better. Actually, this is going to sting a lot, sorry."

It was Chaco.

He took hold of her upper arm near her armpit. She tried to resist, but a pain struck the side of her neck with such force that her whole body seized in fear. She felt, rather than heard, herself scream. Her neck grew hot and then cold, like a very thick ice cream was being pumped into her artery. There were tears on her lips, but she hadn't felt them roll down her cheeks.

After what seemed like an eternity, the pain that had been ravaging Deja from her neck up vanished as if she had stepped into a shower and simply rinsed it out of her hair.

"Oh, my God," she said, her voice returning.

"Better?" Chaco asked, his form now somewhat more discernable.

She felt as though she'd just woken from a perfect night's sleep. "Not only better, I feel great."

"I told you." He leaned over and kissed her forehead.

"What's in that stuff?"

Chaco held up a small pneumatic infuser, about a quarter of the size a doctor would use. "Back at the lab, we call this a 'Neuro Cocktail.'" He tossed the tiny instrument into the trashcan, and it hardly made a sound. "What you were feeling," he said as he stroked the side of her face, "is pretty common after what you've been through."

"How long have I been asleep?" she asked, wiping the tears from her eyes with the edge of the bed sheet. She glanced about and saw that she was in Chaco's room at The Thin.

He hesitated. His eyes shifted to the mounds made by her knees under the blanket. "28 hours," he said, barely above a whisper.

Deja thought she felt the pain coming back. "What?!"

"Don't worry. It's typical for a first-timer." He patted her knees through the blanket and waited for a reaction.

A strange uneasiness began to sink in, and Deja could sense that something was off. It wasn't that Chaco was hiding something: more like he was protecting her. He hadn't said or done anything specific, though. It was just a feeling. She sat up and rubbed the side of her head. "Sonny," she began before she stopped and pulled the blanket up to her chest. "What happened? How did I get here?"

Chaco's smile looked forced. "What's the last thing you remember?"

She tried to recall, but a thick haze of angst seemed to be

blocking her. "Oh, Sonny, I'm sorry. I did something really stupid."

"Shhh," he said and placed a finger to her lips. "Don't worry. You didn't do anything stupid. Now tell me, what's the last thing you can remember? Why don't you start from the night Cor died."

"Okay. I couldn't sleep much that night, so I guess around 5:30 I finally got up. I walked down to Bar of Soap and ordered some breakfast. I remember I was reading *The Times* – something about fashion – when Marl suddenly appeared and scared the shit out of me. I guess it was in my head, because that weird waitress said I was talking to myself." A slight ache returned to Deja's head, so she rubbed her temples.

"It's okay, baby. Go on."

"He asked me to meet him in your Net conference room. I know it was dumb, but there's something about him that makes me think he's got a plan. So I called Pavia's brother. I thought he'd let me use that virt chair of his. I figured he'd still have the coordinates in his system." A memory surfaced of the chair's tentacles, which caused her to bury her face into the palms of her hands.

"Hey, easy there," Chaco said. "Come on, tell me ... what happened next?"

"I got to Bartas's, and I ... I don't remember anything after that." Fear gripped her as she suddenly recalled the creepy look on Bartas's face. "God, Sonny, Bartas didn't do anything sick, did he?"

"No, no he didn't. In fact, by what I could tell, he was trying to shut the chair down."

"Is he all right?"

Chaco hesitated, and then shook his head.

"Is he dead?"

"No, but he's going to be in a Neuro ICU for a long time. It's probably just as well. He was pretty bad off. Maybe they can do something for him."

"Sonny, how did I get here?" Deja had woken confused about the night before plenty of times, but the issues surrounding this question were different. Just the act of asking it unnerved her.

"I had Tsuka find you on the grid, and when I got to Bartas's, I shut the chair down before you got any deeper into the Net. That chair's powerful. If you're not used to it, it can mess with your nervous system. By the time I got there, you were already unconscious. I called in a med team for Bartas. I woke you, but you were still pretty out of it, so I brought you back here to the room. You don't rember that?"

Deja shook her head. Another memory of the tentacles flashed across her mind. She began to rock slowly on the bed. "Was Marl anywhere in the Net ... when I was in?" she asked.

"There were no signs of his presence. At least, none that I could find."

"I wonder if he's still here ... on the planet?"

"I doubt it. We checked, and he's definitely off the grid. I had Tsuka go to his hotel room, but it's clean. No prints, no DNA, nothing. It's like he was never there. Whatever he is, he's beyond our technology. I'd sure like to meet the people who made him."

Deja still felt like Chaco was protecting her from something, but she couldn't imagine what. Anyway, it didn't really matter, because all she wanted was to forget about Marl and Bartas and Pavia – the whole fucking thing for that matter. Deja always knew getting involved with a government agent might mean things could get a little crazy, which, to be honest, was the main reason she started dating Chaco in the first place ... to add some excitement to her life. But if someone had told her that within a year she would be siphoning data to the government, witnessing death by Light-Force, and possibly dialoguing with an alien life form, Deja wouldn't have believed it. She bit her lower lip and began to rock harder.

"Hey, don't worry, I'm not going to let anything bad ever happen to you." Chaco placed a hand to her shoulder. "You're safe now, and I'll bet you're pretty hungry, too."

Deja suddenly realized the tightness in her stomach. "Yeah," she said, rubbing her belly, "I could eat a hamburger."

Chaco laughed. "You *are* hungry." He walked over to the door of the bathroom and gestured. "But before I order us some burgers, you need a little pampering." A soft light flicked from within and cast the tip of his nose and the rim of his brow into hot yellow edges. "I thought you might need this."

PAUL BLACK

Deja gingerly walked from the bed to Chaco. She was in one of her camisole tees and a pair of panties, though she couldn't remember putting them on. She could tell her hair had been washed because it was free of its usual stiffness. She slipped her arm around his waist and peered into the bathroom.

Around the large whirlpool bath were dozens of tiny candles, and the room smelled like that quaint toiletry shop they had stumbled into during the last day of their Paris trip.

"Sonny, thank you." Deja kissed him before she crept up to the tub and dipped her finger through the bubbles. She turned and smiled, then removed her camisole and panties and tossed them into a corner. She carefully stepped in and slipped under the water.

Surfacing, she wiped the bubbles from her face to find Chaco kneeling by the side of the tub. He was staring at her as if she were a fragile doll. Not in an overly protective way, though – just genuinely concerned. It made her feel safe and protected.

"How are you feeling?" he asked.

Deja leaned back and guided a generously large bubbleburg across her chest. "Great, considering I've been in a coma for over a day. Why?"

Chaco didn't respond. She sensed her answer had brought some kind of relief for him. She scooped up a handful of bubbles and began making him a puffy goatee. He took her hand, kissed it, and nestled it to his cheek.

"Oh, Sonny," she said, cradling his face, "you're sweet to be this concerned. Don't worry. I'm not going to fall all to pieces over Cor." She tenderly kissed him. "I'm a strong girl," she whispered.

Chaco laughed slightly. "So I've been told."

No questions

MEATBALL shot off the counter like he had been fired from a pneumatic cannon.

Chaco turned the blender off. "Why are you acting like you've never heard this before. *Meat?*"

The cat darted under the bed so fast that his tail slapped the edge of the metal frame.

"What a 'fraidy cat," Chaco said and resumed making breakfast, which today consisted of a spoonful of protein powder, a banana, two cups of plain yogurt, and a bag of frozen, genetically improved strawberries.

He poured the mixture into a tall glass and took a gulp before he collapsed onto the couch and stared at his New York case file. Its unchanging position relentlessly reminded him that it had been two weeks since he had returned from his assignment. With Slowinski still out on medical leave, he had procrastinated way past the brink of departmental acceptance and had entered a time frame that could get his ass in a serious crack. He picked up the file's Netpad and scanned through its folders. Losing all trace of Marl, failing to connect Goya to the rest of the case, and the disappearance of AztecaNet's top security man had paralyzed him. He couldn't bring himself to complete his report. The whole Corazon issue, he hoped, would work itself out. And he sure as hell couldn't bring up the "close encounter" thing; it was definitely a career ender. "Hell," he said and flipped it shut.

Meatball emerged from beneath the bed and began stalking Chaco's foot under his baggy sweatpants. The cat pawed and caught the tip of his big toe.

"Damn it! You little asshole!"

Meatball retreated across the loft's concrete floor and skidded to safety under the bed.

Chaco examined the blood oozing from the tiny puncture and pressed a paper towel against it. "Meat, shit. Don't you ever do that—"

"Sir, you have two Netcalls," announced the loft's HDI system. "One is marked high priority, the other urgent."

"What are their IDs?" Chaco asked, dabbing at the wound.

"Ms. Deja Moriarty and Yoichi Tsukahara."

Chaco glanced at his watch. 11:09 a.m. *Shit*, he thought, *Tsuka probably screwed up his ADR's again.* "Send Deja's through and transfer the other to my NSA message box."

Deja's holo-image formed to the left of the coffee table. She was in her office, her arms folded tightly across her chest. There seemed to be a commotion behind her. People were darting past the opening of her cubical. She started to speak, hesitated, then brushed her hair back in a way that meant something was up.

"Morning," Chaco said while he took another swig of breakfast.

"Turn on INN *now*," she said.

"Request. Give me INN, full screen."

The Ansel Adams image of Cathedral Peak that hung on the wall opposite the couch dissolved into a locked-off shot of the United Nations main assembly hall. It was framed by an INN info banner ticking off submessages and vid-pulls from six correspondent remotes. The UN was in full session, and nothing looked all that unusual. But Chaco almost dropped his protein shake when the camera cut to a close-up of the main speaker.

It was Marl.

He stood behind the podium smiling that familiar smile of

his and wearing the same coat, which appeared fairly normal in the harsh camera lights. As the INN image sequenced through various angles, Chaco saw that a U.N. security detail had rushed the stage, only to be stopped about 20 feet from the podium. They were frozen in various positions of attack, some with their weapons out and aimed at Marl. The rest of the assembly appeared able to move, but most had chosen to remain seated. A few were standing and looking around in confusion. It all seemed surprisingly calm, considering that Marl had suddenly materialized in the seat of the most powerful governing body on the planet.

Chaco looked at Deja.

She raised an eyebrow.

"What the hell is he doing?" he asked.

"Changing the world?" she replied.

"Wasn't Alberts speaking to the assembly today?"

"Yeah, but two minutes before she was supposed to take the stage, Marl just materialized."

"Jesus. Has he said anything yet?"

"We've checked all of our feeds, but so far he's just standing and grinning. He's been there about 15 minutes. Wait, go to INBC!"

Chaco scanned through the different news networks and stopped on INBC's feed from outside the U.N. A dozen armored personnel hover-carriers were touching down on a blocked off street. As each one landed, about 20 heavily armed Special Ops types jumped out. A series of quick-cuts showed close-ups of the troops securing the area. The image cut to a female correspondent standing in the street across from the U.N. As she described the scene in trite network adjectives, two imposing, black tractor-trailers edged their way through the chaos behind her. Chaco had heard of these trucks. Their conspicuous lack of markings, along with the complex array of antennas atop their roofs, confirmed to him that the OST had arrived.

He sighed. "See those black trucks? This is going to get ugly."

"For the sake of us all, I hope it doesn't. What are those, anyway?"

"Probably MCC's for the OST."

"MC what's for the who?"

"Mobile Command Centers for the Office of Special Tactics. They're a section of DoD. Technically, they don't exist, but a buddy of mine was once recruited by them and–"

"Go back to INN!"

INBC's image cut to a medium shot of the podium before Chaco could react. As he scanned back, he found all the Networks were carrying the same feed. The camera was dramatically slow-zooming while Marl gazed out to the assembly hall. He had that heavy look Chaco had seen before, but this time it was tinged with an air that seemed paternal.

"Here it comes," Deja said.

An icy ripple went through Chaco. It was the same feeling he had back at The Thin when he was holding Deja on the night of Corazon's death. Something shifted across his heart, as if an old part of him had slid away to expose something new ... something he had been suppressing for a long time. He looked at Deja and could tell she had felt something, too.

"I love you," she mouthed.

Chaco felt his lips answer her with the same words, but a silence had settled around him. He looked back to the vidscreen and realized that the world was about to change forever.

The camera locked-off on a tight shot of Marl's face. As if on cue, he looked directly into the lens, gave a slight smile, and slowly closed his eyes.

When Chaco's vision returned, he was back in his parent's old yard in Hooker. Marl was standing not five feet away. This time, there was no wind – just a clear sky and a perfect temperature. Chaco was still dressed as he had been in his loft. He curled his toes into the dirt but didn't feel any texture or mass. Even the cut on his toe was gone.

"Hello, Sonny," Marl said casually. He wasn't wearing the coat anymore. He was dressed in a black t-shirt, faded blue jeans, and a pair of old Nike cross-trainers designed by an aged fitness guru. The shoes were wildly popular until the guy's face fell on national TV during a live infomercial. Marl even sported one of those stupid med watches that changed colors with your cholesterol level. It all seemed vaguely familiar, like everything had come from the Super Walmart in Hooker. But even though Marl looked remarkably normal, Chaco knew he was just a conduit for something greater; behind his blue eyes was unthinkable knowledge amassed from an ancient race that had probably evolved into wisps of non-corporeal energy.

"Hello, Marl. Nice clothes." Chaco was surprised how calm he felt, considering he was dialoguing with a creature that could wield power at the speed of thought.

Marl leveled a look that penetrated to the core of Chaco's being. Chaco didn't feel any fear, however. There seemed to be a benevolence emanating from Marl, as if he were about to explain the meaning of life or something.

"Please, Sonny, don't be afraid," he said. "At this moment, I am speaking to every human on your planet, just as I am to you." Marl's attention shifted slightly, and it felt like he was looking right through Chaco. "Many of you are asleep and will think that you are dreaming, but rest assured this is not a dream. Many of you will likewise be concerned for the safety of your passengers or patients or others in your care. Do not worry. The length of time we will spend together will be imperceptible. It will not affect your judgment, abilities, or anything in your environment. When I am gone, it will be as though you had blinked.

"Let me introduce myself. I am a messenger. The ones

who set into motion the variables that gave way to the rise of life on your planet sent me to help your world evolve. When I am through, this conversation will be part of your new collective consciousness. I was sent to put your world into balance by implementing an effect that would bring order to your cultures. Usually, this effect would go unnoticed by your world, but after studying your people and their complexities, I have concluded that the only way your cultures will put aside their differences and come together as a world community is to discover that they are not alone in the universe. Believe me when I tell you that this is the truth.

"Mankind's potential is vast, and with respect to the universe, you are just infants. But even as infants, your future is yours to create, so I suggest that you start by helping your own. Only then can you begin to travel a path that will elevate your species to a new order. This revelation will spawn many questions within your different cultures, religions, and governments, but is not this the essence of evolving? It is not our intent to guide you or to become more involved. You already have the necessary tools and capacity to make this journey. The length of time you take will be up to you, but I suggest that you start immediately." His look took on an even more serious quality. "Please be aware, this is not a suggestion. We will return from time to time to check on your progress, and our assessments may have consequences."

Chaco thought he felt a gust of cool air pass over the back

of his neck.

Marl looked about the yard before he centered his focus on Chaco. "Sonny," he said, as if addressing only him, though Chaco deduced 12 billion other *infants* felt the same. "Do you have any questions?"

An odd embarrassment rose in Chaco, and he looked away. Such a simple question. One that a professor might ask at the conclusion of a lecture. Chaco couldn't think of anything, because nothing Marl had said came as a real shock. In fact, it all seemed to resonate pretty true. What he felt now was a mild guilt, as though humanity had always known better but had been too fucking busy being selfish. Now all those Biblical references to man as "children" made sense: as a species, they were infants, and it was about time to finally grow up. Chaco wondered if Marl, at this moment, was engaged in answering billions of questions. But when he looked back, Marl was standing serenely waiting, his hands clasped in front of him.

"No." Chaco looked down and dug his toes into the dirt. "I don't have any questions."

A broad smile came over Marl's face, and he spread his arms. "Then I welcome you, Sonny Thomas Chaco, to the family of the universe." An intense white radiance exploded from his smile and obliterated the Oklahoma landscape.

"... Where's Marl?" Chaco heard himself say.

"I don't know," Deja replied. "He just disappeared from the stage."

Chaco watched as the security detail – released from whatever had been holding them – rushed the empty podium. Many of the delegates had charged the stage, but the Special Ops guys were pushing them back and barking for them to remain calm. The OST marched up in the new offensive combat gear Chaco had heard about – Objective Fabric that could mend a wound in battle. They were leading a team of specialists in bright orange HAZMAT suits. The correspondent was clearly flustered and bullshitting her way through the play-by-play. The whole scene was surreal, and as the OST began to set up a perimeter around the stage, the correspondent gave up and stopped reporting. Her loss of words summed up the situation. Chaco glanced at Deja.

"Hey," he said, "are you all right?"

Deja pulled herself away from something out of the holo's view field, probably the same report Chaco was watching. She faced him with a puzzled look. "W-what did you ask?"

"Are you feeling anything? I mean, did Marl talk with you ... in your mind?"

Deja slowly nodded. "Yeah. It's like I remember it, but it feels like an old memory."

"Me, too. It feels like it's a part of my past. Did he tell you about himself and why he came to earth?"

"Yes, he did."

"Did he mention that we'll have in our collective consciousness the knowledge of his existence?"

Deja nodded.

Chaco whistled. "I guess he did talk with everyone."

Deja turned and stopped a guy walking past her cubicle. They conversed for a moment before she turned back. "Yeah, Sonny, he did because everyone here is walking around in sort of a daze. It's taking time to sink in, I think."

The INBC's report had shifted to a newsroom with six professor-types vidlinked to a moderator. The whole thing looked hastily staged as they roundtabled on various theories about Marl. One professor, a stately gentleman with an ornate handlebar moustache, was sure that his appearance was a new form of holo-teleportation, probably funded by a terrorist group. Another wearing a pair of Net-Linked Micro-Night optics conjectured that Marl was an alien life form here to help the world. His eyes darted back and forth, most likely following the information being fed to him by the Micro-Nights. Another dismissed all of the theories and said Marl was obviously a precursor for the Rapture. What else could he be? One thing was certain: it appeared that all of the professors, including the moderator, now had a sense of Marl's message imbedded in their memories. The Micro-Night guy slammed his fist onto the table and demanded an explanation.

"Sonny?"

Chaco glanced back at Deja's holoimage. She looked very

worried. "Hey, Dej, what's the matter?"

"It's all going to be different, isn't it?"

That was the understatement of the century. "It'll be different, but maybe it'll work. I mean, maybe Marl's intervention will finally get us moving in the right direction. Stop all the bullshit fighting over religion and shit."

"I don't know, Sonny. It's going to take a lot more than a five-minute brainwashing to keep people from killing each other."

"I think he wants us to figure it out. He just supplied the push we needed. Dej, I've got a good feeling about this. I guess it was the way Marl came across. He seemed pretty sincere to me ... kind of fatherly, you know?"

An odd smile spread across Deja's face.

"What's so funny?" Chaco asked.

"It's so weird you say that."

"Why?"

"To me, he came across like my grandmother, the one who raised me. It's not like he looked like her, obviously. It's ... I don't know, he just had this way about him when he was talking to me. It was weird, that's all."

"Yeah, it's like he knew who we would listen to the most, then took on the characteristics of that person."

Their eyes met, and a feeling that was becoming more familiar fluttered across Chaco's heart.

"You know I meant what I said earlier.... Don't you?" Deja asked.

"Yes," Chaco answered, "I know."

Deja gave him a hairy eyeball almost as good as Slowinski's.

"And?"

"What?"

More hairy eyeball.

Chaco chuckled. "Right," he said. "I love you, too."

.

I promise  35

IT felt like she had been inside a dream at the bottom of some distant ocean for 1,000 years. She tried to open her eyes, but a layer of sleep as thick as death pressed against her struggle. Dark silhouettes greeted her as she blinked away the pain.

"Doctor," said a voice, possibly a female's. It was hard to tell.

Another silhouette joined the two already at her side. They whispered across her as she lay in a warm and comfortable bed. The new silhouette leaned down and touched her shoulder.

"This might be a little startling for you, but don't be afraid. We're here to help." A man's voice of soft timbre. "Do you understand?"

"Yes," she heard herself say, the word emerging as if from deep hibernation.

"All right, then," the male shadow replied. "Now, just relax. This won't hurt."

He reached down and removed something she suspected had covered every aspect of her for a long, long time. It passed over her eyes; a light so bright that it stung bloomed to fill her vision.

"Good morning," the man said, now in a low level of detail. He was older with a closely cropped beard, his face filled with sincerity. The other two shadows were Asian women who looked almost like twins with their sharply cut bangs and pale complexions. They shared his concerned look, though somehow not as genuinely. The older man's ID pin labeled him as Dr. Haderous. When she read his name, a torrent of memories threatened to drown her in a wave of pure emotion. Her last memory was standing by her pool, at her home. She had a drink in her hand – her favorite, a vodka martini – and people were standing around the edge of the pool, laughing and talking. Suddenly she stumbled backwards (falling, maybe?) and her drink flew out of her hand. She gasped loudly at the memory's intensity.

The doctor gently stroked her forehead. "Don't worry,

this sensation will pass. What you're feeling is simply your brain coming back on line after a period of dormancy. There's nothing to worry about." He looked away and motioned for someone to join him. The two Asian women smiled shyly, bowed, and shuffled out of view.

A large man approached the doctor's side. His hat cast a shadow across his face, but when he removed it, she saw that his eyes were moist, as if he had been crying. He leaned down.

"Kita, my love," he said with such grace that she instinctually touched his face, "how do you feel?"

Searching his eyes, she could feel his name enter her mind with a clarity that seemed almost too perfect. Then she remembered their life together, and there was a stinging behind her left eye. "Tired, Oscar." Her voice was working now, but mechanically.

"That, too, is typical," Dr. Haderous said. "It's nothing to be concerned about."

"What happened?" she asked, already having a vague sense of the answer.

"You fell into our pool and hit your head," Oscar replied. "You've been in a coma."

"How long?" she asked, surprised at her own calmness regarding the revelation.

Oscar glanced tentatively at the doctor.

Dr. Haderous smiled and patted her shoulder. "Mrs. Pavia," he said in a way that reminded her of her father, "one thing at a time.

What really matters is that you're awake and on the road to a full recovery."

Oscar gathered her hands, which looked like a child's compared to his. She noticed the scars across his knuckles and flashed a memory of his time in the Middle East. "Everything will be all right, my love," he said tenderly. "I promise."

At that moment, for reasons she didn't yet understand, she knew he would keep that promise for the rest of her life.

ACKNOWLEDGEMENTS

I would like to thank the following for their assistance, inspiration and patience: Lisa Glasgow, Bridget Foley, Brian Moreland, Pat O'Connell, and Max Wright...you all were there for me when I needed you.

For future trends in technology: *www.socialtechnologies.com* and its wealth of future forecasts and models of global trends. And to NASA News and the Langley Research Center Web site for its white papers on the future of technology.

Special thanks to my editor and friend, Jay Johnson, for his faith in my talent.

And to Trish, as always, with love.

Dallas, 2010

PAUL BLACK always wanted to make movies, but a career in advertising sidetracked him. Born and raised outside of Chicago, he is the national award-winning author of *The Tels*, *Soulware*, *Nexus Point* and *The Presence*. Today he lives and works in Dallas, where he manages his graphic design firm, feeds his passion for tennis and dreams of six figure movie deals. He is currently working on a new book of fiction tentatively called *The Samsara Effect*.

THE TELS
PAUL BLACK

BOOK ONE IN THE TELS TRILOGY

THE YEAR IS 2101 A new revolution has spread across the human landscape. The
Biolution and its flood of technology have changed almost every aspect of life. Also
changed, is the face of terrorism.

Throughout his life, Jonathan Kortel always sensed he was different, but never imagined
how different, until two rival factions of a secret group called the Tels approach him out
of the shadows of government. He has a gift that could change his life, and possibly the
world, forever.

This is his story. A battle for the loyalty of a man who could change the course of human
evolution. And the struggle inside this man as he comes to terms with his destiny.
Deeply intriguing and powerfully suspenseful, Paul Black has created a future
described as "mind-bending" by the *Dallas Morning News*. Part *X-Files,* part cyber-thriller,
Paul Black unveils a view of a world that could be just around the corner.

NOVEL INSTINCTS
www.paulblackbooks.com

SOULWAR
PAUL BLACK

BOOK TWO IN THE TELS TRILOGY

THE WORLD IS NOT WHAT IT SEEMS For Jonathan Kortel, his life has changed forever. He has a telekinetic gift that is faster than light, and he's now part of a secret new group of humans. They're called the Tels, and they live in the shadows of a future where the Biolution and its flood of technology have changed all the rules.

Having been thrust into a world he cannot control, Jonathan begins a quest to uncover what's really going on in the Tel world. Because he soon realizes that he's not only their star pupil; he's their most important experiment.

Here continues the journey of Jonathan Kortel, author Paul Black's fascinating future character, introduced in his award-winning 2003 novel *The Tels*. *Soulware* picks up where *The Tels* left off, following Jonathan as he discovers his true destiny. Deeply intriguing and powerfully suspenseful, Paul Black has created a vision of the future that is haunting and disturbingly real.

NOVEL INSTINCTS
www.paulblackbooks.com

Available at all online retailers including **Amazon.com** and **BN.com**.

9 780972 600743